HIS VIRGIN PRINCESS

INTERSTELLAR BRIDES® PROGRAM: THE VIRGINS - 5

GRACE GOODWIN

GET A FREE BOOK!

JOIN MY MAILING LIST TO BE THE FIRST TO KNOW OF NEW RELEASES, FREE BOOKS, SPECIAL PRICES AND OTHER AUTHOR GIVEAWAYS.

http://freescifiromance.com

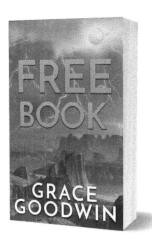

INTERSTELLAR BRIDES® PROGRAM

YOUR mate is out there. Take the test today and discover your perfect match. Are you ready for a sexy alien mate (or two)?

VOLUNTEER NOW!

interstellarbridesprogram.com

1

*D*anielle Gunderson, Planet Everis, Outskirts of Feris 5

THE COLD SEEPED into my bones through the hard ground where I settled. The thin sheets of silver and black thermal blankets kept me from freezing to death. The food I'd managed to steal before leaving the Touchstone was running low. Me? I could survive on less. If I had to, I could build traps and survive in the wild. I'd done it before. But I had no idea what condition my mate would be in. He'd been blocking me, refusing to let me into his dreams, ordering me to stay away from him.

"As if," I huffed.

I didn't dare take off my boots, just shoved them into the bottom of the thin sleeping bag. If I took them off, I'd never get them back on because of all the hiking I'd done. The swelling was so bad in my injured ankle that I could feel my toes turning blue. I propped my feet up on a large rock and sighed. "I will find you, Gage. And when I do, you've got some explaining to do."

Yes, I was talking to myself, something I often did in the woods. But if my mate learned anything about me, he would need to understand that I was no princess content to sit around in silk and perfume at the Touchstone as Hunter after Hunter tried to woo me. Even my friends, Lexi and Katie, underestimated me. Yes, I was smallish. Five-two with shoes on. No, I didn't weigh a lot. But small didn't mean weak, didn't mean clueless. My dad taught me that. He'd only been five-nine, but he'd been a Navy SEAL. When he'd retired, he'd taught me to love the land like he did. We'd spent hours exploring the Florida wetlands and summers wandering in the wild Montana mountains. Until he died, and my beloved mountains turned on me.

But that was another life. Another planet. A life I'd traveled across the universe to leave behind. And damned if I'd let some stubborn Everian Hunter keep me from my happily ever after. Maybe I had a touch of a princess in me after all.

I could track almost anything. A skill I'd learned from my dad. But since arriving on Everis, I'd also discovered that it was an ability of an Everian, that tracking was inherent to those from this planet. I had the mark on my hand, as my father had. According to Warden Egara, back at the Interstellar Bride Processing Center on Earth, the mark proved we were descendants of aliens, Everians, to be exact. I had Hunter DNA in my blood. In my soul, more like. Understanding why I'd never been content to sit inside a classroom, why I'd dropped out of college and returned to the outdoors, had been a relief. My Earth friends hadn't understood the restlessness inside me. It was always there. Urging me to go. To *seek*. To hunt. Something. Anything.

Coming here had seemed like a dream come true, like coming home.

Until my mate decided not to show up at the Touchstone and claim me. He set the mark on my hand – and my body – on fire, and never showed. Big jerk. Then I find out he'd been captured or kidnapped or something and he told me to stay away, not to risk myself, to find someone else. Like I'd want another man to touch me when I knew that man wasn't 'The One'. I'd saved myself for someone special, waiting for sex to mean more than a quick screw in the back of some good-old-boy's truck, and my mate was not going to steal that from me.

No. I could track a mountain lion across a river and over a mountain. I could follow alligators through a swamp. I could find one stubborn, pain-in-the-ass mate. And I was close. There was no way he'd be able to keep me out of his head now. For two days, I'd been walking in this general direction, following something I couldn't explain, even to myself. It wasn't visible, tangible. There were no breadcrumbs to follow.

It was instinct. The deepest part of me demanding I put one foot in front of the other in this direction. I wondered if this was what a homing pigeon felt like, flying, always flying in one direction with no idea why. And maybe no one to welcome it home at the end of its long, painful journey.

I wiped the track of tears from my right cheek and curled into a ball on the ground. My back to the rocks, I was protected from the wind, and the thermal wraps let me get warm enough to sleep. At least as much as the stabbing pain in my wrecked ankle would allow. It was dawn, and I'd been walking all night. Now, I needed a few hours to recover, to rest my old injury, let the swelling go down.

I stared up into the strange Everian sky where two moons hung low on the horizon. The small, silver moon was called Incar, and was the most famous prison in the entire Coalition, from what I'd been told. The larger, pale green moon was called Seladon, and was green because it was covered with life, the entire moon a farm for Everis and its sister planet in this system, Everis 8. I was on Everis 7 now, technically the home world. The Everians referred to the other planet as Eight and had colonized it several hundred years ago. The information I'd read said over a billion people lived on Eight now, and I wondered if humans would ever colonize Mars. I tried to imagine that many people living there, looking back at Earth and never even visiting the world they came from.

The idea made me sad. But I was sad a lot these days. Frustrated. Angry.

Waiting for Gage to come for me had left me with a lot of free time to read, but lying there as the final twinkling stars faded, I was glad. It made this place feel less foreign, more like home. And I hoped, when I found my mate, I wouldn't still think volunteering to be an Interstellar Bride had been the biggest mistake of my life.

I was close. I could feel him now, even when I was awake. His energy called to something primal inside me, and I knew I'd die before I'd walk away. I had no logic for this, so I'd given up trying to rationalize what I was doing out here, miles and miles from the nearest city, alone, freezing, wandering around a series of mountains and caves looking for a man who might not exist.

"Shut up, Dani." I yanked on the covers and pulled them

up over my head, shutting my eyes as the darkness closed in around me. "Just shut up and find him."

There was a difference between tracking him and dream sharing. One I could sense his location and be pulled toward it, but that was all I had to rely on. A pull. Until now when I was close enough once again to be with him in our dreams. He was mine, whether he liked it or not, which meant he had to let me inside his head. He didn't have a choice.

I was done playing little Miss Nice Girl. I had no idea who he was or what his role was on this world. Criminal or saint. Scarred and ugly, or an Adonis. And I didn't care. He was mine.

I closed my eyes and willed my body to shut down, and my mind to find his...

Gage...Dreaming

She invaded my mind like a master, first blurring the edges of my pain with warmth and seductive promises, then luring me from reality to a beautiful land I could never have imagined on my own.

"Danielle." I whispered her name, standing strong and whole behind her. She was dressed oddly, in dark brown pants and a forest green jacket. The boots on her feet were for trekking over rough terrain, but her golden hair was down, the yellowish sun of her world transforming the strands into an ethereal halo. She turned to me and held out her hand, her blue eyes warm and hypnotic.

"Gage. Come to me. See how beautiful my home is." I had to reach out. Our hands touched and she pulled me to stand beside her overlooking a stunning mountain vista, the sparkling blue and white of a raging river far below us. The Hunter within me drew the fresh scent of forest and female into my body like I was starving for it. I was.

"You shouldn't be here, Dani."

"Where is that?" she asked, her smile wicked and alluring and everything I'd ever dreamed it would be. She was perfect, my mate. Full of sass and life and fire. Everything the ladies at the capital were not.

"In my head, mate. Being near. It's too dangerous. Someone wants me dead, and I don't want any danger to come to you." I stepped closer, lifted my thumb to her lower lip so I could trace the softness. I knew it wasn't real. Didn't care. "Dream sharing is all we will ever have."

"I disagree, but now is not the time to argue. It is time to do as I wish." Her gaze raked down my body. Lower. Lower, still. In this dream, I was back to full health, my body strong. Aroused.

"And you shouldn't have any clothes on." The moment the words left her luscious, pink lips, I was naked and realized my mistake. She wasn't in my head, I was in hers, and I was too weak to turn away from what she offered. Respite. After two days of torture and pain locked in that dark cave cell, I wasn't ready to go back. Nothing but death waited for me there. And what I wanted right now was Dani. My Marked Mate.

Her lips traced a heated path from my chest to my abdomen. Lower, until she wrapped her hands around my hard cock and smiled up at me. I noticed a white, fluffy pillow on the ground under her knees and she grinned up at me. "It's my dream, hot stuff."

"I don't believe so." I traced her cheek with my fingertips. "This is definitely my dream, not yours."

"Then tell me what you want, Gage."

Not Lord Gage, or Lord of the Seven, or even my lord. Just Gage. The man. "I want what's rightfully mine."

She licked her lips and pressed her thumb to the tip of my weeping cock as her other hand cupped my sensitive balls. "And what is that?"

I hissed out a breath at the exquisite feel.

"Your mouth, Dani. The first of the three sacred virginities to be claimed by your mate."

"And are you, Gage?" She looked up at me through her pale lashes. She looked demure, but her position in front of my raging cock made me think her a vixen. "Are you my mate? Are you really mine?"

I'd denied her for so long, to protect her, but she'd disobeyed me. Come for me anyway, despite my warnings and denials. She had to be close, close enough to once again be in my head. I had no choice but to find a way to survive, to find her. Perhaps it was the fact that she was cupping my balls, or it was the searing heat of my mark, but I could deny her no longer. "Yes. I am yours, Dani. And you are mine."

"It's about time, you big jerk."

Before I could chastise her for rudeness, that crude mouth was around my cock, sucking me into a hot, wet heaven. I groaned at the feel, the sweet suction as her lips pulled inward. She worked me with her tongue, swallowing me down like I was her favorite treat. The sight addictive. Powerful. Humbling.

How could I love a woman I had never met? Never touched. Never held in my arms?

This was the power of the Marked Mate, the mind-to-mind connection we shared. This was my gift from the gods, and I ached for her. My cock, but more importantly, my heart.

My orgasm was swift, rolling through me like a lightning bolt without warning. I did not fight it, for now it was my turn to feast on my mate's sweet pussy. Even in a dream, I could dominate. To strip her naked and make her scream my name. Only my name.

Lifting her in my arms was easy as she was tiny. So much smaller than me that it was hard to remember the vixen on her knees was so fragile. Breakable. I backed her to a large tree, pinning her petite body and kissed her like the drowning man I knew myself to be, yanking at her clothes as she helped me strip her naked in this untamed land she'd once called home. Her love for the mountains sang through her mind in the dream, the birds singing, water raging, the high-pitched call of a pack of wild things made me pause and tilt my head to listen. Their song was beautiful and haunting, just like my mate.

"Wolves. They're called wolves."

"Are they beautiful?" I asked.

"Very."

I looked into her eyes, held her pressed to me, naked. "I want to see this place. And your wolves."

"Then you will." The conviction in her eyes made my chest ache, and I lowered my lips to hers, claiming her again. Tasting her. Mine. She was *mine*. "You are mine, Dani. Your sweet pussy is just for me and me alone. I claim it. Now. Do you give yourself to me?"

She nodded, the long swing of her hair sliding over her bare shoulder. "Yes."

I lowered her to the ground, shocked to find a thick blanket spread beneath us. The fabric was striped, and soft, warm to the touch despite the chill in the air. "What is this?"

"Flannel stuffed with down. It's from my bed. My dream, remember?"

I settled her on the dark blue and red blanket. "Is this where you are now, mate? In your bed?"

Her gaze grew dark and serious. "You know I'm not."

"Where are you?" I asked. I shouldn't. I knew the answer would enrage me, make me feel helpless. If we were dream sharing, she wasn't at the Touchstone. She was nearby.

"I'm safe. That's all you need to know."

Her words settled me and my gaze wandered back over her curves, the thin line of her body and small breasts. She was not soft, but lean. Strong. So beautiful. The scent of her wet core drifted from her body, made my mouth water. I ran my hand over her breasts. Her curved waist. Her hips. Lower.

"Gage." She arched off the ground as I lowered my mouth to her clit, sucking her essence into my body so I would never forget her taste. Her scent. Carefully, I slipped one finger into her tight pussy and groaned as her body clamped down on it like a fist.

"Mine," I breathed against her tender flesh.

"Yes."

I spread the soft lips of her pussy open to my eyes and feasted, tasting and sucking, flicking her sensitive clit with my tongue as I worked my finger in and out of her wet heat, rubbing the inner walls of her pussy as I expertly pushed her closer and closer to the edge.

Her fingers buried in my hair and she cried out, her scream echoing off the canyon walls below us as she came, her pussy bucking and milking my finger, hungry for my hard cock.

I was hard, even though I'd just come down her throat. Hot. My cock so heavy it felt like I'd hung weights from the damn thing between my legs. I wanted her. Needed her.

Her hair spread out around her head like a halo. Her lips were full and ripe from my kisses. Her pale skin was flushed, her eyes shone with passion, lust, and unrestrained pleasure. She looked like a goddess. My goddess.

"I want you, Dani. To be inside you. To fuck you. Make you mine."

With a smile, she spread her legs, exposing her wet, pink pussy. She might be a virgin, but she knew her passionate nature, didn't hide from it. Or me.

"Yes." She pushed against the ground with her feet, lifting her hips in eager invitation.

And cried out in pain, reached for her ankle. "Damn it!"

Reaching for her, I pulled her into my arms, cradling her, looking over every inch of her small body. "Are you hurt? Did I hurt you?"

"No. It's just an old injury...shit. This wasn't supposed to happen. I'm waking up. I'm sorry. It hurts too much."

"What? Dani?"

The mountain faded. She disappeared and I woke, chained. Bleeding. Dying. Cold. Left for dead in a mountain cave so remote no one would find me in time. My cock? Hard as a rock, but my heart breaking, the imagined taste of her lingering on my tongue.

ani, Planet Everis, Exact location unknown

THERE HE WAS. After hours of hiking since I woke up, my body aching with need from the steamy bout of dream sharing, I finally found him. Followed my innate sense as a Hunter descendant, the heart-sense of a Marked Mate searching for the other half of her soul. My heart was frantically beating out of my chest at the sight of him. I saw the rusty chain affixed to the wall, curling across the floor and beneath him. Light-years from Earth, this was the perfect male for me. Warden Egara and the testing knew it. I knew it. I was sweating from my trek, but I shivered in the cave.

This hellhole. He'd been left to suffer. Die.

No one would have found him. Ever. Only me, only his Marked Mate because of our connection. The mark on my palm flared with heat and I hissed at the feel of it. A moan came from his injured form, knowing he felt the same sensation. My presence.

I closed the distance between us and pulled the huge drop bolt from the rusted metal cage door holding him. I threw the long chunk of heavy metal as far as I could and pulled the door open, dropping to my knees before him. My ankle screamed a protest, but I ignored it completely. I'd survive, but Gage? I wasn't sure the extent of his injuries.

He sat on the hard ground, his back to the bare stone behind him. Chains hung from well over his head, outside the cage, out of reach, the dark metal links attached to manacles on his wrists. He was asleep, or unconscious. I wasn't sure which, his body limp and his arms loose, manacles in his lap. His face, god, his beautiful face was bruised, his lip swollen, blood soaking his hair to run down his temple. I reached out, cupped his shoulder. He was cold, his bare chest covered in blood and burns, his skin like ice. They'd left his pants on, but his feet were bare as well and freezing. A thick jacket was on the ground just out of his reach. It was the same style the Hunters wore at the Touchstone, although filthy.

"Gage." When he didn't respond, I shook him. "Gage!"

I knew he was alive, knew because of the mark, his response to our marks being in such close proximity.

"Dani?"

"I'm here. Come on, wake up."

I felt him stiffen, perhaps finally realizing he wasn't dreaming, that I really was before him, urging him to move.

"Dani?" he asked again, this time his eyes cleared, widened. He groaned through gritted teeth. His dark pants were torn everywhere, dried blood clearly caked into the fabric in multiple places. I took a better look at his torso, the power and muscle covered in cuts, burns and blood. He looked like he'd been through hell, but I had no idea if everything was superficial, or if he was bleeding on the inside, too. Broken ribs? Bleeding kidneys? He was a mess, and seeing him injured made every cell in my body scream in denial.

He was mine. This could not be allowed. "You're a mess."

"Why are you here?" he countered, drawing his knees up toward his chest. We stared at each other, our gazes roaming. He was big. So very big, even sitting with his knees tucked up. His dark hair was long enough that it curled slightly over his ears, was thick, and I wanted to bury my fingers in it, learn the texture of him. A beard had begun to grow on his square jaw. Even in the dim light that came from the cave entrance, I could see the color of it was a touch redder than the nearly black hair on the top of his head. His lip was not only swollen, it was cut and bleeding. His face was thinner than in my dreams, as if he hadn't eaten enough for a few days, but his eyes pierced me, held me in place. A predator's eyes. Focused completely on me, taking in every detail, missing nothing. His gaze lingered on my ankle, on the tilt of my hips as I kept weight off it. It was like he could read my mind, knew my body already, was attuned to me.

His eyes were almost black, piercing in their intensity. I recognized him, not just from the dreams we shared, but in my heart, in my very DNA.

He was studying me just as closely and lifted his hand to reach out to me, but he let it drop.

"Are you real?" His voice was rough, dry. "Or am I dreaming?"

I tugged off my backpack, pulled out a canteen, removed the lid and handed it to him. "Real. Drink."

He took it, swallowing the water greedily. How long had he been in this cave? Had he not had any food or water in days? As he drank, I glanced about. He'd been left in an abandoned cave, large enough for four or five men to walk side-by-side. I could easily stand at the entrance. If I put my arms up, I wouldn't be able to touch the roof. The floor was stone, dirt and dead leaves covering the cold gray rock like a rotting carpet. We were about fifteen feet from the entrance, the daylight muted by the thick stone walls. I could hear water dripping in the distance, a gentle plop, plop. The chains holding him were large, heavy, but old and rusted, stained by the patina of age. The metal loops and bolts in the walls had been in place for a long time, as if Gage wasn't the first to be brought here. To be tortured and neglected until dead.

A cage in the middle of nowhere? For what? "What kind of monster keeps a place like this?" I wondered aloud.

"My great-grandfather," was his answer and it brought my gaze back to him at once. He smiled, but there was no humor in it. "This is my cave, Dani. Ironic, is it not?"

"Not." I grabbed the discarded jacket and wrapped it around his feet. "Definitely not. We have to get you out of here."

He used the back of his hand to wipe his mouth. "I will ask again, what are you doing here?"

I frowned. "Saving you."

He shook his head slowly. "You shouldn't have. Too risky."

"You were going to die."

He met my gaze. The vein his temple throbbed. "I know."

"Then—"

He lifted his hand, but it dropped back to his lap, as if he were too weak. I reached in my pack again, found some kind of protein bar in the military rations I'd taken from the storage room at the Touchstone and handed it over. "Eat slowly."

Breaking off a piece, he put it in his mouth, chewed. I watched the simple action, the play of his throat as he swallowed. Reaching out, I took his free hand, turned it over.

There.

The mark.

I placed my palm in his, mark to mark for the first time.

I gasped at the feel of it, the all-consuming burn throughout my body. Heat and need flared to life, but now wasn't the time. But I also felt complete. As if a part of me had been missing...forever. I had no idea how I'd gotten through life, going through the motions. Perhaps it was that I hadn't known I wasn't whole.

But now...now there was no going back. Gage was mine and he could yell at me until he ran out of steam and I wouldn't care.

"Someone wants me dead." He shoved another piece of the bar in his mouth, chewed. "I won't have them after you."

"I can take care of myself. And as for you dying? Not happening."

He moved his shackled wrist, the chain rattling. "As you can see, I'm not going anywhere. I've had days to try to figure out how to get out of here."

I dug through my bag again. "I picked up some things at

the Touchstone that might be helpful. A communication device." I placed the small object on the ground, but he quickly reached for it.

"Picked up?"

I gave him a quick glance, then went back to my task. I wasn't going to tell him I stole them. My intention was to *borrow,* to return them when I'd rescued Gage and we returned together. Better to beg forgiveness than ask permission, especially when I knew those cavemen would never have let me come along. And they wouldn't have been able to find him, not without me. And the mark that called to me like a homing beacon.

"A comms unit? How did they not track you down within a mile of the Touchstone?" he wondered.

"It's not turned on. Obviously. I removed the power cell. I didn't want anyone to be able to follow me, because knowing my friends, once they got their mates involved, they would have come after me. Stopped me."

"Who are these mates you mention?"

"Hunters at the Touchstone."

"They should have stopped you. I will discuss this failure with them in future."

I frowned, pursed my lips. He should be thanking me, not pissing me off, but I'd give him a little latitude, for now. Mark it up to him being delirious. And since we were in a cave...well, I guess it made sense he was acting like a caveman. "Well, I'm here. With a comms unit. And this."

"Fuck! An ion blaster?" he cried, grabbing the weapon from me, checking the side of it. I had to assume he was looking for the safety, ensuring it was on. "You could have shot yourself."

I huffed out a breath. "You're not mated to an idiot. I

know how to use a gun. How to shoot. How to carry one safely so I don't shoot myself. If you haven't caught on by now, I tracked you. I'm not a city girl, Gage." His gaze narrowed, but he remained quiet. "No one else found you, did they?"

He exhaled, stared at me almost grudgingly, realizing I was right. I was here, saving his ass. Settling the blaster into his hold, he slowly stood, aimed the weapon at the plate on the wall above our heads where the chain was securely affixed just outside the bars.

"Get behind me."

I moved as he wished, but his arm came about and all but shoved me farther back.

The shot echoed off the cave walls, as did the heavy clink of the chain as it hit the ground. I looked around his body, saw that he was no longer connected to the cave wall. "Another." He aimed at his wrist, about three chain lengths above the shackle. "Wanted to test it first. See what happened. I'd like to keep from shooting my hand off."

He fired again, one length of chain falling to the floor like a dead snake. The other was still attached to the shackle on his opposite wrist and I realized he'd been hooked up to some kind of pulley system. He put the ion blaster in his opposite hand and fired a third time. I sighed in relief when the entire length of chain clanked against the cave wall as if it were dead. At least that's how I liked to think of it. He still had shackles around both wrists, but he was mobile. One problem at a time.

Gage turned to me, tipped up my chin. "Let's get the fuck out of here."

He put his jacket on, taking what little warmth he could from it. He moved toward the entrance and I followed.

Slowly. Thinking out loud. "We can't walk back to the Touchstone. It's too far. There's not enough food or water. While I can forage for both of us and hunt for meat if I have to, you're weak. Injured. We don't have time for that."

"You are injured as well." He looked down at my ankle, as if he could see that it was swollen inside my boot. In the daylight, I could see the olive tone of his skin beneath the blood, the fullness of his slightly darker lips, the play of shadows over his very ripped, very muscled chest and back. Holy hell. Hottie. Score one for me. His deep, rumbling voice made me shiver, and not with cold. "Did you bring a ReGen wand?"

I frowned. What? "I don't know what that is."

He sighed, then smiled at me for the first time. "That's all right. You've done a good job. Thank you."

I returned the smile with one of my own. "Now that I found you, we can call the cavemen for help."

"Cavemen?"

"The mates of my two friends from Earth." I pulled the comm unit from his hand and reached into my pack for tools—which consisted of a carving knife I'd stolen from the kitchen—and the battery—or whatever they called the odd lump of metal I was placing inside the unit to turn it back on.

"Your friends are mated to Hunters who live in caves? I have never heard of such Hunters. Not even in the old lore." He slowly shook his head as he took another bite of the energy bar. "I do not believe we should summon strange cave dwellers to our aide. Someone wants me dead. If you hadn't found me, they'd have accomplished their task."

"Who?"

He shrugged his broad shoulders. "I have no idea." He

looked up at the sky, closed his eyes. Breathed deep. It was as if he'd expected never to see the sun again, to feel fresh air on his skin. "We can't trust anyone."

"Not even your friends?" I asked. "Your family? Do you have a family?"

He reached out, stroked a finger down my cheek. "I am a member of the Seven. On Everis, this is a high-ranking position. I am known throughout the planet. My family has held the seat for thousands of years, passed from generation to generation, but I am the last of my line. I have many enemies, Danielle. Any number of people could be involved in this. I do not wish to get my father's mate or my sister involved. It's too dangerous. As for friends? I don't have friends, only those who want something from me."

"That's terrible."

"It is as it has always been." He grunted his agreement, but didn't say more. I disliked that he was resigned to this. Not a fun life.

"Well, I have friends. We'll call Katie and Lexi. They're also from Earth. They've only been on Everis for a short time, just like me, and I promise you, they aren't part of any plot to kill you. They don't even know who you are. Hell, when we volunteered, we had no idea we would be matched to Everis. You can trust them."

"I do not know them."

"Do you trust me?" I asked, looking up at him.

He straightened, as if I'd insulted him. Puffed up his chest. "You are my Marked Mate. I trust you implicitly. You are the only one."

I put my hand on his arm. But not liking the cold, stiff cloth separating us, I slid my palm down until our hands, our marks, touched.

"Then trust me in this. Katie and Lexi will help. Their mates—Elite Hunters—will help."

"I don't know. They sound suspicious, and not worthy, living in caves. How do they properly care for their mates?"

I laughed, I couldn't help it, the Earth-girl reference to caveman mentality obviously was not translating well through Warden Egara's handy NPU. "They don't actually live in caves. On Earth, that's what we call a man who is overly protective, dominant and bossy."

"Who is we?"

"The women."

This made him grin for the first time, and I knew I wanted to see humor in his eyes a lot more often in the future. "Then they sound like excellent males indeed, for that is how I intend to be with you. Overly protective, bossy and definitely dominant."

I batted my eyelashes at him, the first real smile on my face in what felt like forever. "Do you know what happened to cavemen on Earth?"

He pulled me close, pressing our bodies together in a warm embrace that was so much more than an introduction. It was a homecoming. When he bent his head and his lips lingered in the wild, tangled mess of hair just above my ear, I could feel his smile. "They kept their mates safe and protected and very, very naked so their beautiful, small Earth females did not go a single day without experiencing wild, carnal pleasure at their masters' hands?"

"No." Holy shit, was my pussy wet and aching? Now? In a hellhole cave with my mate injured and bleeding and days of filth and sweat coating both of us? Gross.

He groaned in my ear and pulled me closer still, until I could feel the large, hard length of his cock. "That is what will happen to you, Danielle, once we escape this place and you are healed. I will claim you in the sacred order of three, learn every single secret your body would try to keep from me. I will make you beg for release and scream with pleasure. I will kiss every inch of you, mate. Claim you. Make you mine."

Sweet talker. "As soon as *I'm* healed? You're a mess. I'm fine."

"No. You are not. And as soon as we have a ReGen wand available, you will be seen to."

"What about you?" I pushed back, staring up—way up —into his dark eyes.

"My wounds are nothing compared to yours. You will be tended to first."

Was this guy for real? He could barely stand. He was cut and bleeding from so many wounds I couldn't count them all. Freezing. Starving. And he was worried about my stupid ankle? "My ankle injury happened months ago on Earth. It's nothing. Just sore from too much hiking."

"You will be tended to first. This is not a negotiation, Danielle. Refuse me and I will spank you for disobedience, as I should right now for your presence, and defiance."

"I saved your life."

His gaze went from intense and sensual to hard in an instant. "And risked your own."

"You could try being grateful."

"I am grateful that through some miracle of the gods you found me and survived. You are never to do anything this reckless again."

"Shit. I thought Von and Bryn were bad."

"Commander Von? Of the Elite Hunters?" His tone changed once more, from annoyingly arrogant and bossy to inquisitive. Trying to keep up with his rapid mood shifts made me feel like a silly cat chasing a dot of light from a laser pointer. Jump here. No, there. No...

"Yes. Von and Bryn are both Elite Hunters. They are mated to my friends, Katie and Lexi. I told you this already. They are the people I think we should call. I trust them." His face relaxed into a semblance of calm, even though I could feel the coiled tension in his body as he constantly scanned our surroundings, listening. Paying attention. But so was I. And I wasn't half dead. We were well and truly alone out here. "Do you know them?"

"I have heard of Von in the council meetings. Not long ago, we sent Bryn on a very sensitive mission."

"Yeah, to Rogue 5. That turned out to be a cluster fuck." I frowned at him, but my disapproval was nothing to his reaction.

"That is highly secret information, Danielle. A very delicate political matter. How is it that you know these details?"

I rolled my eyes. "Katie is Bryn's mate, remember? And she's one of my only friends here. She almost ended up claimed by that Styx guy. And that would not have been good."

"Our operations on Rogue 5 are highly secure. It is not good that we have had a breach of protocol. He took his mate with him? Bryn will be held accountable."

"And I thought Von was a hard ass," I mumbled. Was this guy for real? He was half dead and worried about protocol?

"I believe you said Von was a caveman."

"Yeah, well, he's a rules-following kind of guy, which makes him a hard ass...*and* a caveman." I took a step away from him but my ankle buckled. I threw out my arms to steady myself, but Gage was there first. Before I could catch my breath, I was in his arms, being carried like a child. "Put me down."

"You are injured. You will not walk until you are healed."

"You're ridiculous. Put me down. I walked miles and miles to get here, Your Majesty. I can manage just fine."

"No. And I am not a majesty. I am a prince. A descendant of the original Seven."

I sighed and gave into the inevitable, leaning my head back onto his shoulder and absorbing as much warmth as I could. "Whatever you say, caveman."

"Soft ass."

That one made me blink. "What did you just call me?"

"You break rules, not follow them. Therefore, you must be a soft ass." His hand drifted down to my backside and started a massage that quickly made my eyes roll back into my head. God, if he ever got me naked, I was in trouble. Do anything he wanted, wherever he wanted, whenever he wanted kind of trouble. "Definitely soft."

"That's not a word."

"It is now." He continued his massage and I didn't even try to hold back the contented sigh. He was safe, not dying —at least not at the moment—and my ankle did hurt like a son-of-a-bitch. But the main emotion making me limp was relief. I'd found him. We were together now. Everything else would work itself out. It had to.

"Use that comm to call Von, and get us out of here, please."

"How far away are these Hunters?"

I managed a small shrug. "I don't know. They're at the Touchstone. But they've been pretty busy with the whole 'three virginities' thing since they found their mates. They're past that part now, but they're not stopping. They might not be...available right away." I felt the heat climbing my cheeks as I tried to explain the obvious to Gage. He must have heard something in my voice, for his gaze was transfixed on my face and there was hunger in his eyes. Fascination.

Possession.

I'd seen that look on the other Hunters' faces when they found their mates. And as much as it made me feel like a stupid, romantic, love-sick idiot, seeing it on Gage's face made my heart race and my mind go blank with longing. I wanted him to look at me like that when he could actually *do something about it.*

He considered my words. I was patient, giving him time. I didn't blame him. Someone wanted him dead. Based on his job, it could be many people. Too many. He didn't want to end back up in a cave like this again.

"Fine. We'll call your friends. Get their help as soon as they can tear themselves from their mates."

There would be no *tearing away.* Lexi and especially Katie were not the stay-at-home type, but I didn't say anything. He'd learn the truth when they got here. Assuming they came for us.

They had to come.

I used the comm and got Katie. No surprise that Bryn took over the call within seconds, demanding my location. I didn't tell them about Gage. When Bryn assured me they were on their way, I disconnected. "I figure it's safer if we don't say your name over the comm until after they get here."

He nodded, warmth filling his eyes as he studied me. "You are an interesting female, Danielle. I will trust your friends, but for now, we alert no one else." He lifted his gaze from me to look out over the horizon, and I saw the Hunter within him for the first time. Hard. Cold. Relentless. "The ascension ceremony is in a few days. Until then, we will need to be careful."

"And after?"

"After, I will scour this planet with Hunters loyal to me until the traitor is taken care of."

3

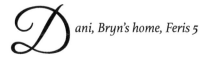

ani, Bryn's home, Feris 5

I WAS in the biggest bath tub I'd ever seen. It could be classified as a hot tub on Earth, but it wasn't quite as scalding. And this one was *in* the bathroom, not outside. It was actually *in* the floor. The water was warm, had some kind of scented oils that smelled like the outdoors and I had the best view.

Gage was in the shower, the thing they called the bathing tube on Everis, and soaping up his torso. He had zero inhibitions, not one ounce of modesty, for he knew I was watching him.

Von and Bryn had responded to our comms immediately. After Gage explained what had happened, they'd readily agreed he needed to remain in hiding. Whoever wanted him dead had to think they'd succeeded, at least for now. Until there was time to unravel who was involved.

Bryn offered his home as a place for us to recover and hide. Since he and Gage had never met, had zero connections other than having mates from Earth, Gage felt comfortable enough with the option. There weren't many available. As a leader of the Seven, Gage had a very public life. I imagined him to be like a famous person on Earth, where everyone knew the moment he sneezed.

That was why we gave Bryn our coordinates and he showed up, Von, Lexi and Katie in tow, in a shuttle. That was the term he called it. Me? It was like a tiny space ship out of a *Star Trek* movie. Transporting across the galaxy from Earth was one thing; I hadn't been conscious. This? I'd been awake and in awe. Sure, I'd just found my Marked Mate, saved him from a certain death, but I was in a space ship. Flying over Everis. It made me realize we definitely weren't in Kansas anymore.

And when Bryn handed Gage a handheld metal rod that glowed blue and apparently healed injuries when waved back and forth over them, I was in technology overload. But when Gage crouched before me and waved the wand over my ankle and the pain lessened, then eased entirely, I was amazed. And annoyed. He'd been tortured and left for dead and he wanted to heal my ankle? The idiot! I'd convinced him I was fine—it would always swell and ache even after a space wand was waved over it—did he use it on himself. It was hard to tell his cuts and bruises were healed based on the blood and dirt covering him, but he perked up, the tense lines of his body and around his mouth eased.

And now that we were settled into Bryn's house—his big, huge, amazingly large house—we were alone. Bryn had pointed to where Von and Lexi would stay and Von hoisted his mate over his shoulder and carried her off. I doubted I'd hear from them again, unless it was sounds of them fucking carrying down the long hallways.

Once we were alone in our suite of rooms—it wasn't just one darn room, but three along with the bathroom with the huge bathtub—I became modest. We weren't dream sharing. Gage wasn't in danger. He was healed and whole and right in front of me.

By the look in his eyes, he'd wanted to touch me, kiss me, and a whole lot more. To pick up where we left off in the dream before my stupid ankle had woken me up. But there was no way I was letting him get near me until I showered. I was all for spontaneous, wild monkey sex, but I didn't want to smell like a monkey when we finally got naked in real life. I didn't want him to see me with greasy hair and stinky armpits for our first real kiss.

He'd turned on the water for the tub to let it fill while I cleaned myself in the shower first. Then I could relax in the deep water. I wasn't going to argue with that, and so I'd nodded. He'd walked out and left me alone...until a minute after the shower shut off. Then, he'd knocked and entered. My body was shielded because of the deepness of the tub and when he'd looked at me, standing so darn tall and dark and handsome, my insides did melt a little. And other places, too.

I'd thought he'd want me to turn around, but no. A slow smile spread across his face as he'd shucked off his filthy clothes, exposing inch by glorious inch of his hard body. Perhaps he was a touch leaner than usual since being left for dead, but he still looked incredible. Broad shoulders, tons of olive-colored, toned skin. He had black hair on his chest, a smattering of it that tapered down to his navel—an innie—and then to a thin line that went beneath his pants. And when he'd pushed off those pants, I'd discovered he didn't wear underwear. He was also very erect and when he saw me ogling, he grew harder. Longer, the bulbous head curved up toward his belly and...whoa, that was going to fit in me? Everywhere? Just because I gave him a BJ in a dream didn't mean it was going to fit down my throat. Or in my bottom.

My nipples hardened and my inner walls clenched at the thought.

Only when I realized I was staring, wide eyed, mouth open, had I looked away. My cheeks flushed as hot as the water in the tub. He'd turned, went into the bathing tube and started scrubbing. And the view from behind wasn't half bad either.

Now, watching him lather up those muscular pecs and dense thighs had my ovaries jumping for joy.

"Do you have family worried about you?" I asked.

His hands stilled on his belly and I wished I could climb in and wash him myself, run my palms over every inch of him. I was sure he wouldn't mind, but I wasn't quite there yet. I had no clue what I was doing, and I didn't want to make a fool of myself. At least not until after our first kiss.

"My mother died when I was two. I don't remember her at all."

"And your father?"

"He has been gone for nearly a year. The ascension ceremony is scheduled to take place on the anniversary of his death."

"I'm sorry." I was. I could practically feel his pain radiating from him. Such a strong body. Strong, warrior spirit. Seeing him hurting was worse than feeling the pain myself. "What was he like?"

"He was strong. Honorable. A member of the Seven. A true prince. I can only hope to live up to his legacy."

"As a prince?" Did he mean that in the *I'm from a royal family* way, or was that just a title they gave high level politicians on Everis? I had no idea. But I was no princess. I felt more comfortable in hiking boots than a tiara.

"As a man." He stood proudly, staring at me, the hunger in his eyes so intense I would swear I could feel his touch from across the room. The water ran over his healed body, dripping and following every curve. Every shadow. Lower. God, he was magnificent. Huge. Everywhere. I glanced up to see he enjoyed my inspection. Without doubt, I didn't have the acting ability to hide my lust for his perfect body.

"What about other family?"

"My parents weren't Marked Mates so my father mated a second time. Again, not a Marked Mate."

"I heard finding your Marked Mate is rare." I moved my hand across the surface of the water, playing with the few bubbles, trying like hell to ignore the heat coming off my mate, and not the physical kind. I'd never wanted a man like I wanted him, and the wait was making me edgy, hyper-aware of everything. The coolness of the air on my shoulders, the heat of the water, the popping of bubbles on my sensitive nipples.

"It is. Very rare. My father died almost a year ago. What is a mate of your parent called on Earth?"

"Stepmother or stepfather."

"Then I have a stepmother, Mauve, and a stepsister, Rayla, who is three years younger than I. Rayla was from

Mauve's first mate, who was killed hunting a bounty on a Prillon criminal."

"No other brothers and sisters? Uncles? Cousins?"

He shook his head, turned and tilted his head back to wash his hair. It was shaggy, a slight shadow of beard on his face making him look dark and dangerous and sexy. So sexy. I devoured him with my eyes.

"No. None. I am the heir to my father's seat on the Seven. My family descends from the original ruling families. I am a prince to my people, and you, Danielle, will be their princess."

Princess? Me? Dani from Florida. A princess? Insane.

I had to look away to form a coherent thought about something besides being the central character of a Disney movie. I couldn't even sing. I was too skinny. Too small. I didn't have the curves to fill out that kind of dress. I didn't talk to mice, or birds, or any other kind of creature. I hunted deer and ate them for dinner. I didn't talk to them or dance in the woods singing songs to squirrels. I wasn't regal or refined, and the ridiculous wave I saw the royals do on television back on Earth would give me carpal tunnel. Seriously? What were we talking about? Me? Royalty?

No.

Family. Right. I cleared my throat and pushed all *princess* thoughts aside. "I don't have any family either. I don't remember my mother. She didn't die, she just decided she needed to go back to the city. She left when I was four, to go off with the yoga instructor from the recreation center in town. I heard they got married and moved to California."

Gage was lathering his hair now and I ended my words. Watching him was more interesting than my worthless mother. And it wasn't just his gorgeous face I was ogling.

With his arms up, his back arched and in profile, his cock thrust out and up from his body. I couldn't miss it. I licked my lips, remembering the soft feel of the skin, the taste of the bead of fluid that came from the tip in my dreams. How hard it was. Hot. How it pulsed against my tongue.

"And your father?" he asked.

I felt the familiar pang of sadness when I thought of my dad, but I no longer felt lonely. My heart was slowly being filled by Gage.

"My father died last year. He taught me everything I know about surviving in the wilderness. He was a hunting and fishing guide. Took people into the wetlands to hunt, to the rivers to fish. We spent at least two months in the mountains up north in Montana every summer. He was a good man. A great father."

The shower shut off and he opened the tube door. Came out. I stared as he walked to the tub, his body dripping with water, his muscles flexing and bunching as he moved with confidence. Ease. Even with a big club between his thighs.

"I am sorry that he has passed on to be with the Gods."

I blinked furiously. I would not cry now. So, I nodded.

"Before my mark flared to life, I was expected to marry Rayla," he said, and I was thankful he moved back to his soap opera life. "The royal engagement has already been announced."

My mouth fell open. Definitely soap opera. "You're engaged to your *sister*?"

He grinned as he slid into the tub, sank down until his shoulders sank beneath the water and moved right in front of me. Placing his hands on the edge of the tub on either side of my head, I was pinned in place. "Not by blood. She is well-loved by the people, a commoner who would become a princess. She is kind and selfless, involved in many organizations that help the common people."

Holy shit. He did *not* just use the word *common* in relation to his sister. *Stepsister*. Whatever.

"Is she beautiful?" I wanted to smack myself for asking that, but the damn words popped out before I could rein in the little green monster roaring to life inside me. Jealousy was a bitch, and I really didn't want to hate my future sister-in-law.

"Yes. She is." He lifted his hand to my hair, held a strand in his fingers as his gaze dropped to my lips. "But not as beautiful as you are."

I blushed; I couldn't help it, not with him looking at me like he was ready to pounce. I wanted to yell at him to hurry up, but I was trapped like a deer in the headlights, frozen. Waiting for him to touch me. Worried he still wanted someone else. "Does she know? About me?"

His gaze softened, drifting to my lips. I struggled to breathe. "Yes. She was thrilled."

I frowned. "She was happy to not become a princess?" That did not compute. No one could be happy giving up this gorgeous hunk of man.

"Yes. We were both trapped by duty. Now she is free to marry for love, not obligation. I love her, Danielle, she is my family, mine to protect."

"You love her?" Gah! Could I sound more like a babbling idiot? But it was completely his fault. I couldn't think. Not with the heat of his body rolling over me like a drug. And his lips. I was staring. *Starving.* I'd dreamed of him night after night, lost him, found him, but he'd never been mine. Real. Not like this. And the hunger roaring to life inside me wasn't normal. It was terrifying. Too much. Too strong. I was spinning out of control, my body not my own, but his. Aware of his heartbeat, the pulse at the base of his neck. God, his scent was like a drug, filling my entire body with heat.

And the thought of him with another woman? The part of me screaming about that was wild and raw, edgy and feral. I'd never felt like this before. I was afraid to move, afraid if I moved one muscle, I'd lose control and pounce. Mark him. I wanted to rub my body all over him, like a fucking cat claiming territory, marking him with my scent— because I knew the others would smell my skin on his, know that he was mine. It was wrong. Strange.

I couldn't stop wanting to do it anyway.

God, maybe I was an alien, because this was innate. Instinct. I felt like the Hunter now.

We were no longer dirty. No longer hurt.

"I love her as a sister and nothing else. But it is nothing compared to how I feel about you. I am your family now, Danielle, and you are mine."

Shaking. Can't breathe. Can't breathe. I needed him to touch me. Needed it more than I needed oxygen. I licked my lips, pleased when his gaze followed the gesture and his eyes grew dark with heat.

"Prove it." I glided through the water and pressed my body to his, chest to chest, lifting my fingers to run through his hair as I'd been longing to do.

The first contact was like a jolt of electricity, my body crackling with heat and lust and want. It was his turn to freeze, to fight for control. Closing my eyes, eager for a taste of him, I pressed my lips to his, claimed his mouth in a kiss.

I was gentle. Soft. My lips lingered. Pulled back. It was an invitation that I knew he wouldn't even try to resist. I wanted him. Needed him to touch me, to make me feel like I truly belonged to him after fighting so hard to be with him. But I wasn't experienced. I didn't really know what else to do except give him permission to do anything he wanted.

No. *Everything,* he wanted. Everything we *both* needed.

I broke the kiss and wrapped my arms around him, holding him tight. Close. As close as I could get. Fighting back a tidal wave of emotion, of love and longing and lust and a million other things I couldn't process, let alone name. I fought back the tears building like walls of fire behind my eyes and pressed my lips to his ear. "I need you, Gage. Please. I need to be yours."

"You are mine." His arms came around me and he held me there for long minutes, both of us fighting for control, both of us trembling, our breaths ragged. His arms were like bands of steel around me, and I'd never felt safer or more connected to another being. Was this love? I didn't know. Love felt like such a tame word for what I was feeling. This was obsession. Devotion. Need clawing its way through my body like a wild animal, threatening to tear me open from the inside.

He held me until my trembling passed, until I relaxed in his arms, content to let him hold me, his hands roaming my back, tracing my curves, learning my body as I surrendered to his touch.

"Have you ever been with a man, Dani?"

"No. Not in the way you mean." I was grateful that my cheek rested on his shoulder, that he couldn't see the dark crimson heat I knew stained my cheeks. "I kissed a few boys in high school, but never...you know."

"Then my first objective will be to wipe the taste of all other men from your lips."

Whoa. But that wouldn't be a big deal. It wasn't like any of those fumbling...

I didn't finish the thought as Gage's hands lifted to cup the back of my head and he gently lifted my face to his once again. His touch was gentle, but the kiss was not. His lips claimed ownership, his tongue diving deep to taste me, conquer me. Make me forget who came before.

Melting. That was the only way I could describe what happened to my body. I kissed him back, the deep moan that came from the back of my throat a sound I didn't recognize. But he did, his mouth became more aggressive, more demanding, and I gave him everything, eager to taste and be tasted.

He tore his lips from mine and lifted me to the edge of the tub so I sat facing him. Panting. Ready for more.

His hot hands lifted to my knees, slowly pushed them apart. "Spread your legs, Dani. I want to claim what's mine."

My knees were wide before my brain could scream a protest. I wasn't like this. I was *not* this wild, uninhibited lover.

But I was.

With a grin that made my nipples pebble and my pussy throb, he placed a hand between my breasts and slowly pressed me back until my back was on the smooth tiles that lined the tub area. I expected to feel cold, but there were towels laid out, thick and soft, and I realized he'd been planning this moment from the beginning. Had thought of my comfort, even as he...

"Oh, god." The words burst from my lips as his mouth clamped down on my clit. No sweet seduction, no slow build or teasing. He sucked me into his mouth like I was candy, then fucked me with his tongue, his groan, the trembling in his hands all the proof I needed that he wanted this. Wanted me.

Mouth on my clit, tongue flicking over the sensitive nub, he slid one finger deep into my pussy, filling me, and I gave up trying to watch him. My head fell back on the towels and I arched my back, lifting my hips, buried my fingers in his hair, silently begging for more.

He worked my body like a master, and I held nothing back as the world exploded again and again, my pussy clamping down on his finger like a fist, the muscle spasms making me sob, then beg, then scream. It was too much. Too intense, the feelings that coursed through my body overwhelming. My ears tingled, colors danced behind my closed eyelids.

When I had nothing left, when I was shaking and spent, my voice raw from screaming, he slid his finger from me, kissed my clit and pussy gently one last time and pulled my sated body from the edge back into the water and into his arms. Held me to him, arms wrapped about me, as if he was what kept me from floating away. His smile was filled with pure male satisfaction, but his eyes held something more. Something tender and real I'd never seen before. I couldn't look away. "Gage," I whispered.

With a soft order for me to hush, he lowered his lips to mine, the spicy taste of my arousal on his tongue making me wild once more. The dazed, sated feeling faded and I *hungered*. I had no idea if this was the Everian in me coming to life, the Huntress needing her mate, but I needed to know his true taste. I needed to conquer him as he'd conquered me.

I spun us in the tub and he let me have my way as I kissed him. Devoured him, pressing him back until he was where I had been moments ago, his back to the edge. "Out, Gage. It's my turn."

He said nothing, but the lust in his eyes was pure, aroused male as he lifted his body and sat on the edge of the huge bathtub. He didn't lie back, and I was grateful. The water running over his rock-hard chest and defined abs made me want to follow the trail with my tongue. So I moved close and did just that.

Rising up onto my knees, I reached for him, kissing him one more time before tracing a drop of water from his neck, down, over his collarbone. His chest. I lingered, tasted his hard nipple. The musky scent of man, *my man,* filled my head, making me dizzy. These huntress senses were overwhelming. Powerful.

Heaven.

My entire being filled with his essence. I drew him into my lungs. My gaze lingered over every inch, making sure the ReGen wand hadn't missed any bruises or cuts. I recalled a particularly bad burn and some black bruising I'd seen over his right ribs. My hand traced the lines of his body, inspecting him as my gaze followed suit.

"I am healed, mate."

"Hush." It was my turn to fuss. To worry. To reassure myself that my mate was alive and well. Whole. Mine. I kissed the area where I knew the wound had been, over and over, telling him without words how important he was to me. He groaned, his hands coming to bury themselves in my wet hair, not to hurry me, but to connect us, to acknowledge my gift.

When I was ready, I worked my way down over his stomach, admiring every inch of this Elite Hunter and his hard body. He was too beautiful to be real. Definitely too beautiful to be mine. But I wasn't going to argue with fate, or Warden Egara's matching protocols, not now. Not when the hard tip of his cock was inches away from my lips.

I licked the tip, the drop of pre-cum glistening there. That was mine, too. He was mine. All of him.

"Dani." My name was a plea and I was only too eager to give my mate what he needed.

As he had done, I was not gentle. I swallowed him down, took him into my mouth with an aggression that shocked me. But his growl, the shift of his hips, the tightening of his fingers into fists in my hair let me know he was under my control now. Mine, just like in the last dream we'd shared.

Wrapping my hand around the base of his shaft, I worked him with my mouth. My lips. Sucking. Licking. Tasting him. He was silk over steel. Big. Hard. I gave a moment's thought to how this huge cock would feel in my ass. Stretching my pussy. The very idea made my pussy ache, my breasts feel heavy and full, my breathing quicken. I'd just come, yet I wanted it again. I needed more.

God, he tasted perfect. Wild and musky and all man.

I took him deep and lifted my free hand from his thigh to his balls, rubbing and playing with them. Claiming them as well. They were mine. His seed was mine. I would carry his child. I would be his everything.

My name burst from his lips, his hands buried in my hair held me to him as he came, his seed spicy, different. Mine. I swallowed it down, every single drop.

Spent, he slipped back into the water and pulled me into his arms. He held me like that for a long time, neither one of us speaking as his breathing slowed, his heartbeat calmed. We didn't need to talk.

When I was a wrinkled, pruned thing, he lifted me from

the tub and dried me off first before tending to himself. The pattern continued as we readied for bed. He made sure I brushed my teeth. Watched as I combed and braided my hair. When I asked for pajamas, he frowned and refused, saying we would always sleep skin to skin.

That was just fine by me.

And when he wrapped himself around me, every hard line of his body pressed against mine, and we drifted to sleep, for once, I didn't feel the need to dream.

4

age

THE BED WAS SOFT, the sheets cool and smooth, the pillow like a cloud. The sun was bright and it felt so good to be—

Dani!

My arm slid over the empty space where she'd been all night. My Hunter senses went on alert. She was gone. I launched myself from the bed, peered in the bathing room. Empty. Turning, I practically ripped the bedroom door from the hinges and sprinted down the long hall of Bryn's home.

"Dani!" I shouted as I went, my feet slapping on the cool wood, the soft carpeting as I ran. Coming out of the hallway, I stopped, practically skidded at the edge of the center room of the home. A comms unit was on the wall and a large seating area faced the screen. I recognized the official news and information channel on display, the talking head known all over the planet as a beautiful, highly intelligent and respected female of our race, but I only had eyes for Dani.

There she was. My heart was in my throat, my breathing ragged. My mark throbbed. She was nearby. If I hadn't panicked, I'd have sensed her, known she was close.

Dani, Lexi and Katie were all sitting on a large sofa, their backs to me, obviously watching the news. Their heads whipped around at my shouting and bold entrance. Kate and Lexi stared at me, eyes wide, mouth open.

Dani shifted about so she was kneeling, her elbows on the back of the sofa. Her hair was loose and down over her shoulders and I remembered what it felt like tangled around my fingers. She wore a pale blue shirt, the neck high, the sleeves long. She was well-covered, but I could see the hint of her slight curves. But in my mind, I knew what was beneath. The small, upturned breasts, the pale pink nipples. The creamy skin.

"Um, Gage, are you all right?"

I put my hands on my hips, looked down at the floor and took a moment to calm myself even more. That was when I realized I was stark naked. "Fuck me."

"She already did that." The one called Katie called over her shoulder in a sing-song voice I found far from amusing. Dani laughed and threw one of the small pillows at the other woman's head.

"Behave."

Katie laughed. "Bryn wouldn't like it if I did."

"True," Lexi supplied, but she didn't turn away from the screen as the other two laughed. Dani's happy eyes locked with mine, and the love I saw beaming there knocked the air out of my lungs. No one had ever looked at me like that.

With a grin, I spun on my heel and went back to the bedroom to get dressed. I never acted this irrationally. Reactionary. Insane.

It was all because of her. I knew her scent, her taste, the sounds she made when she came. I knew everything I needed about her. The rest would be discovered over the course of our lives.

I just had to wonder if I would ever calm down, would ever get past this feeling of panic at her absence.

I doubted it. I looked around, tried to figure out where my clothes were when I realized I had none. Only the ruined uniform I'd worn when trapped.

"Fuck."

Stomping over to the bed, I ripped off the sheet, wrapped it around my waist, and went back down the hall, kicking the long tail of it out of the way.

"Dani!" I shouted again. This time she met me at the end of the hallway. She stood before me—I could see she had on black pants that were rolled up at the ankles—with a smile on her face that she wasn't trying very hard to stifle.

"I have no clothes," I growled.

"You're awfully cranky when you wake up," she replied. "Not a morning glory, then?"

"Time of day is irrelevant when my mate isn't in bed with me."

She clucked her tongue, went up on her tiptoes to kiss me. She was so tiny, so much smaller than me that I leaned forward to meet her lips.

I growled, wrapping my arms about her, pulling her in for a real kiss. None of this peck on the mouth shit.

I didn't stop, didn't lift my head until I heard Von growl. "Put some fucking clothes on."

I felt Dani's smile as she pulled away. "Um, Gage. You're naked again."

"I don't care. I have you in my arms."

"I care," Bryn growled. "I don't want my mate to see your junk."

Sighing, I put Dani back on her feet, reached down and picked up the sheet I'd let fall to the floor and wrapped it back around me again. "It's not my fault your *junk* isn't adequate for her needs."

Bryn laughed. "Nice," he replied, his tone sarcastic. "Come with me, I'll get you something to wear."

I cupped Dani's chin and she nodded. "I'll be right here."

"Where did you find those clothes?" I asked, my gaze roving over her.

"They're Katie's. A little big, but at least I'm not naked."

I growled then, low and deep, thinking of Von or Bryn seeing her bare. Seeing what was mine.

"Gage," Bryn said, prompting me to follow him.

With one last look, I turned and followed the Hunter down a labyrinth of hallways until we came to the master suite. I stood just inside the doorway as he walked into his closet and returned with a handful of clothes.

I dropped the sheet and dressed. This time, Bryn offered no complaint, only leaned against the wall and asked. "Who do you think is responsible?"

I knew to what he was referring. "I have no idea," I tugged on the pants, knew that since I didn't wear underwear he wasn't getting them back. "Someone close to me had to have given them my location. Someone on the inside. Most likely one of the security detail, but that team is vast. One of us." The pants fit well and I adjusted them on my hips as Bryn sighed.

"We're looking for an Elite Hunter. And one assigned to the Seven. If you're right, he won't be an easy target."

"No, he will not."

Silence stretched as my mind listed possible suspects. New guards. Old. Men I'd known and trusted for years. None were above suspicion, not with Dani to protect.

Bryn cleared his throat. "Not to sound like an ass, but I don't pay much attention to politics. Who would benefit the most from your demise? As prince, and the last of your line, your death would completely change the dynamics of the Seven. There would be an epic battle for power to claim your seat. I assume you have enemies."

"Many." The list was indeed long, some family rivalries dating back hundreds of years, but not blood feuds. As far as I knew, none had stooped so low as to assassinate a member of any royal family, not in centuries.

"So, who wins if you die?"

I shrugged. I had spent many hours in the cold, dark cave thinking of little else. "I am the last to carry the bloodline. The only heir. If I died, as you said, a massive shift in power would occur. There are several families who might be strategically positioned to claim my familial seat on the Seven."

"What about your sister? Can't she inherit the seat?"

My denial was instant. "No. Rayla is a sister by marriage, not by blood. Her mother, Mauve, married my father when Rayla and I were both very young."

"Well, that's not helpful," he muttered. "Is there anyone you *can* trust?"

I shook my head, sure that my face looked as grim as I felt. "Danielle. Mauve and Rayla. And now you. Von. Your mates. No one else."

"Short list."

"So be it." I thought of Dani, of her golden hair and soft skin, and something dark and feral rose up within me, snarling at the threat to her. "And I do not like the idea of my mate being in danger. But I have the ascension in a matter of days. By Everian law, the ceremony must occur, or my claim is forfeit. Dani must remain here, where she is safe, until this is resolved. I hate to part from her, but while I am her Marked Mate, I am also a prince. I have a duty to my people."

His chuckle caused me to lift my chin and glare, which only made his smile widen.

"I do not envy you. As for Dani remaining here? She sneaked out of the Touchstone, Gage. She took food and weapons, clothing and gear, and none of us could track her. She found her way into the air ducts and littered the entire building with clothing she'd worn so her scent would randomly appear and disappear when the different sections kicked on and off. If you think I can keep her here, you're wrong. She outwitted an entire building of Elite Hunters. There will be no keeping that woman anywhere she doesn't want to be. And based on the way you had her screaming her pleasure all night, I assume she will want to be by your side. Or under you."

He grinned, slapped me on the shoulder.

A dark rumble went through my chest. Ferocious pride and a depth of fear she would put herself into such risks. "I don't want her to be in danger. That is not acceptable."

Bryn crossed his arms. "I understand. I didn't want Katie following me to Rogue 5, but she did. And she saved me, in the end."

"No." The thought of Dani, my Dani, in danger was

unacceptable. "And your breach of protocol on Rogue 5 will be discussed before the Seven upon my return."

He slowly shook his head as he crossed his arms over his chest. "Hard ass 'til the end, Gage? Take it up with Katie and see how far you get."

"You don't deny the breach in security? Your failure to follow protocol? Endangering your mate?"

Bryn had the good grace to look sympathetic instead of amused as he walked to me and settled a hand on my shoulder. "These are Earth women. Marked Mates. They're different. Trust me. You can't win this battle. Dani *will* follow you. She's got Hunter blood. She tracked you when no one else could. It's better for you to keep her close, where you can maintain a watchful eye on her. The safest place for her is by your side, not chasing after you all alone."

I growled at the image he painted. Dani alone, in potential danger, all because she was adamant to be by my side and I refused. Giving myself a moment to control my ire, I shrugged on the shirt. Bryn and I were of similar size and it fit well.

"I would like to have her close," I admitted. "But it is not to be. I return to a life of politics and enemies. I am used to the attention, the pressure. But Dani, she is not. I do not like the idea of putting her on display for the world, of making her a target. Not yet."

"She's safe, for now. I assure you this home is well-fortified. I'd do nothing to put Katie in jeopardy. But you can't hide Dani away forever. You must find the culprit and eliminate him. While there could be others, you and Dani must live the life you were both destined to live."

"But Dani—"

"The marks prove she was destined to be your princess.

You must let her fulfill that role. It's her destiny, Gage. Not just yours. Not anymore."

I knew his words to be accurate, but I felt the sharp bite of fear of something happening to Dani. "Will it lessen? This need to protect? To claim?" I asked.

Bryn stepped back and his shoulders relaxed, the corner of his mouth tipped up. "Hell, no. No one will hurt Katie. No one," he growled. "As for claiming? That need hasn't lessened yet and it will only do so when I am dead. I assume you've not completed the Sacred Order of Three?"

"Not yet, but now that we are together, I anticipate the claiming to be finished by dawn." I thought of how she'd writhed beneath my hands, my mouth, in the tub. She was so responsive, passionate.

Bryn grinned, pushed off the wall, slapped me on the back as he stood beside me. I'd slipped on my socks and was ready to return to our mates. "One night? You sure you want to give her that long?"

I laughed, followed him back to the main room, my mind spinning with the thought of taking her back the bedroom and claiming her second virginity now. Perhaps that was a better idea. Complete the ritual, claim her ass, today, before we had to return to my home in the capital and everyone would want a piece of me again. Bryn's logic was sound. Before I left, I'd make sure she was one step closer to being mine forever.

Her shocked gasp halted my thinking as I entered the sitting area. All three women were still seated on the large couch, watching the screen. The face on display one I recognized well.

"She's so pretty," I heard. It wasn't Dani, but Lexi, Von's mate. "I can't believe they were engaged."

"She's his stepsister. It was kind of an arranged thing." Dani shifted in her seat, but I heard the doubt creeping into her voice as Rayla spoke from the garden in front of my ancestral home, begging for my safe return.

The large comms display changed as the news feed showed clips of me with Rayla and my stepmother. They showed even older images of me when I was a young man standing next to my father. Seeing his smiling face made my chest ache all over again. Only now that I had Dani did I understand what hell he'd survived when he'd lost my mother, been left to raise a son alone.

The screen changed back to that of my stepmother. There were lines of strain around her eyes and mouth and she looked older than when I'd last seen her. Exhausted. Yet her voice was clear and strong as she stood, holding Rayla's hand offering a reward for any information leading to my return.

At the bottom of the display were the words 'REWARD FOR MISSING PRINCE'. And a staggering number of credits.

"Holy shit. He's a prince?" Katie asked.

"Does that make you a princess?" Lexi immediately asked.

I waited, sensing unease from my mate that I did not like. She was staring at Rayla and my mother. Their clothing was of the finest quality, their hair perfectly arranged and jewels and marks of their station as members of my family adorned their necks. They were beautiful and elegant, a stark contrast to the wild thing wearing borrowed clothing, her lips still pink and flushed from my kisses, her hair a wild tangle I couldn't wait to touch.

She licked her lips and took a deep breath. "Crazy, right?

Me! A princess. I won't ever look like *that*." The whispered words felt like a confession from the deepest part of her, and there was sadness in the words. Acceptance.

"Mate," I said, my voice deep. Clear.

All three females whipped their heads about to look at me.

"Do I have to spank your ass so that you remember that you are the one I want? The one my mark calls to? The one whose mark proves she is the princess she was born to be? The most beautiful woman I have ever seen? The only female on any planet I will ever desire?" I walked forward slowly and placed my fingers under her chin, gently lifting her face up to meet my gaze. "The woman whose sweet pussy I tasted last night and hunger to taste again?"

age

SHE GASPED and turned bright red as her friends laughed. Bryn slapped me on the shoulder as he walked by. I released my mate, but not before I made sure she saw the promise in my eyes. *Later,* I thought. *We'll finish this conversation when my cock is buried balls deep and you no longer doubt who you belong to.*

"See that man beside Rayla?" I asked, pointing my finger at the big display.

"There are three of them. Which one?" Lexi asked.

"The two men with dark hair, Geoffrey and Thomar, are my mother's most trusted guards. They served my father before his death. Now they serve Rayla." Lexi nodded. All three of them did. "Do you see the man with golden hair, standing directly behind my sister, his body between her and the others?"

"Yes," Dani said as she nodded.

"That is Elon. He is the leader of her personal security team and the one she loves. I assure you, her eyes are solely on him. Especially since he most likely claimed her first virginity by now, tasted her pussy and made her beg for more before letting her come."

Dani popped up, jumped over the back of the sofa with the easy grace of a true Hunter and placed her hand over my mouth. "Stop talking about tasting pussies."

I grinned against her fingers, then wrapped my arm about her, scooped her up and carried her to a large, comfortable looking chair where I dropped down, settling Dani on my lap. "I only care about one pussy, mate. Yours."

She blushed further.

"If she's in love with that Elon guy, why is her mother going on and on about the two of you being betrothed?" Katie crossed her arms and arched a brow at me. Bryn leaned a hip against the couch directly behind her, the warning on his face making me choose my words carefully, despite her disrespectful tone. Bryn was right. These Earth females played by rules I did not yet understand.

But I would learn. My arms tightened around Dani.

"We have been betrothed for the last two years," I admitted. "As I had no Marked Mate, the union was a politically powerful one that would cement the status and wealth of both families. But when my mark came to life, and I shared my first dream with Danielle, I told Rayla the truth. I would not keep something like that from her. It was not fair, kind or something I wished to have looming over me as I went to the Touchstone to claim my Marked Mate."

Dani's shoulder settled under my chin and she rubbed her head against me, seeking comfort as her friend, Lexi, asked a question. "Did you break her heart?"

"Not at all." Lifting Dani's face to mine, I placed a chaste kiss on her lips and held her gaze. "She confessed her heart belonged to another, to Elon. She was overjoyed to know Danielle existed, that she would be free from the betrothal. As was I."

Dani's blush, and the softness radiating from her, was more than enough reward for the confession. She smiled shyly. "I just...I'm sorry. I had no idea I could be so...jealous. I don't really know anything about you. And they aren't talking about Elon, they're talking about *you*. Your betrothal to someone else. Does your stepmother know about me?"

"Here on Everis, there isn't the term stepmother. When my father married her, she became my mother, even if she didn't birth me. But yes. Of course I told her about you, that I was going to the Touchstone to claim you."

"Then why are they still talking about you and Rayla like it's a done deal?" Lexi asked. "And that Geoffrey guy, he looks a lot like you, especially when he scowls like that."

I chuckled, staring at Geoffrey. It was not the first time someone had mentioned other Hunters who resembled royals, but he was a Hunter born in my home city. We both had dark hair and dark eyes, but that was where the similarities ended, except for the scowl, which I was quite proud of. As Hunters, looking fierce was part of the job description. Lexi's other question, however, bothered me and I stared at the screen, working through the possible explanations I could give to my mate. But I was saved as it was Von who answered. He'd been observing everything silently from the edge of the room. "It makes sense. More sympathy when it's a beautiful, young princess begging for the return of her one true love."

Dani nodded and returned her attention to the screen, although I felt her tense muscles. She was not happy I was betrothed to another, even if it was all for the benefit of the media and politics. "Totally true. She looks devastated."

Indeed, Rayla did not look well. Her usual glowing complexion was pale, and she had dark circles under her eyes. The normally bright green color was surrounded by red instead of white, her eyelids swollen as if she'd spent many, many hours crying. "She cares about me, *as a brother.*" I added the last to reinforce I only wanted Dani.

Katie snorted, the sound oddly cynical coming from a woman. "Yeah, well, that monster-sized reward is going to motivate a lot more people to find you than a sappy, spoiled princess will. Trust me."

"You're such a pessimist," Lexi accused.

"I'm a realist, honey. You should try it sometime. Get your head out of the clouds once in a while." Katie's grin was suggestive. "Get down and dirty with the rest of us."

"Do not dare." Von leaned down and claimed Lexi's mouth in a kiss that made Dani sigh, and my cock harden before he pulled away. "I love you as you are."

Lexi's smile was blinding, trusting, completely lacking in guile, and I looked away, uncomfortable with the obvious display of devotion. Dani was mine. Without doubt. But she did not look at me like that—with absolute love and complete trust. Not yet, and I was shocked at just how deeply I hungered for it. I glanced down at my mate.

"You wish to know about me, then you shall. With pictures." I pointed at the display again, where Rayla and her mother still stood. "That is Mauve. My mother. As I said, stepmother, on Earth."

She had the regal bearing of a member of the royal lineage. Indeed, she was a descendant of the Seven, a distant cousin to another sitting council member, but still treated like royalty, especially after she married my father. Not born to the role of princess, she had embraced it fully in her years with my father. She liked the status, the fame, the power behind my job more than I did. The fact that both she and my father had told me their marriage was political and not based in love had kept me from embracing her as a true mother, no matter how she'd tried to play the part over the years. And she had tried. But I had been young and stubborn, and too full of my own importance to accept her as a true mother.

"They still believe you are missing," Bryn stated. He sat beside Katie, pulled her into his side and lifted her legs over his lap. "Although, we don't know who *they* are."

Dani stiffened in my arms. "You have to tell them. Mauve and Rayla have got to be making themselves sick with worry." She pointed at the display. "Look at them."

"Your sister looks like she's about to drop," Lexi added. "Poor thing."

"I still say, one comm call and we're rich. Then you two go back to your palace. No harm. No foul." Katie's words were ominous, but there was laughter in her blue eyes.

Bryn silenced her with a kiss. "I am already wealthy, mate. You need for nothing. Mind your manners. And don't forget, whoever did kidnap Gage is still out there."

"Yeah, bee-atch. Our best friend is about to be a princess. You better behave," Lexi added.

"Where's the fun in that?" Katie asked.

"Who you calling a bitch? As princess, I'll throw you in the dungeon, woman." Dani laughed and I relaxed, realized her friends were teasing her. No, teasing us.

It was an unusual, but not unwelcome, experience.

Dani looked up at me. "We do have dungeons, right?"

Smiling myself, I made my face stern. "With viper pits and diseased rodents to chew the meat from her bones should she ever threaten you again."

"Gross," Lexi blanched and reached for Von's hand.

Katie threw her head back and a burst of glee filled the room. "Bring it on, *Your Majesty*."

My mate settled into my arms again, her smile still there, but tempered by worry as she returned her attention to my sister's tearful face on the screen. "Well, dungeon master, we better figure out what to do, because I don't think your sister is going to last very long looking like that."

"No, she is not." We watched in silence until the report was over and the screen returned to the normal cycle of news. Planetary shifts. News from the front and the war with the Hive. Crop reports from the farming moon of Seladon.

Life. I could have died in that cave and nothing would have changed. The universe would move on. Time stood still for no man, not even a prince.

It was humbling, but it also made me realize just how precious my life was to me now that I had Dani in my arms. She offered a future brighter than anything I had dared imagine. A Marked Mate was rare. She was truly a gift from the gods, one I would die to protect and was honored to love.

"I must tell my family that I am well. I do not want them to suffer. I must do that in person, when I return to the palace."

"What?" Dani stiffened and pulled away to look up at me, a storm brewing in her blue eyes. "What do you mean, when *you* return to the palace?"

I cupped her face. "I will go soon. Tonight. The ascension ceremony is fast approaching." I looked down at my mate, who was biting her lip to keep from interrupting. I found the move adorable. Enchanting. I kissed her. "After the ceremony, you will follow me to the palace, and we will announce our mating to the world."

"But you don't know who tried to kill you," Dani stated. "It could be anyone, even the royal guards."

Bryn's gaze lifted to Von's, who nodded. "I can call in the Hunters from the outpost at Feris 5. We have fifty Hunters there, men who fought with us in the Hive wars. Men we trust. I will go to them and bring at least a dozen here to escort you back to the palace. It shouldn't take long."

"Escort him?" Katie asked. "You mean escort us. *All* of us. There's no way I'm missing my BFF becoming a princess." She raised a brow, her gaze darted to Dani and that grin widened to a full-blown smile but it was me she addressed. "And if you think your new mate is going to sit here like a pet dog while you go back to face your enemies, you don't know Earth women very well, *Your Highness.*"

No one had dared speak to me in such a tone, not since my tutors had chastised me when I was a boy. But Dani was agreeing with her and Bryn gave me a telling look. Earth mates were stubborn creatures. He *had* warned me.

"Danielle, I don't think..."

Her hand came up. "Don't *Danielle* me. Stop talking now. I am not staying here. Not happening."

"It's not safe in the capital."

"It's not safe anywhere, Gage."

I sighed, regretting the necessity, but knowing I had to do what would keep Dani safe. "I will give orders for you to be confined to the bedroom, mate. It is only for a few days."

"I'll be gone in a few hours, Gage. And when I track you down, I will *not* be happy."

"Dani, please, be reasonable."

She held up her hand, mark toward me. "I found you. I saved you. I escaped from the Touchstone under all of their Elite Hunters' noses. I am a hunter. Make peace with that now or we are going to have problems, baby."

Baby?

"We will take enough men to ensure their safety," Von said. "I would feel better with our mates close."

"Where we can keep an eye on them," Bryn added, sharing a look with Katie that I was sure had a vast amount of history behind it. Based on what I'd heard about her following him to Rogue 5, I was almost afraid to ask.

"Very well." We would all have to go. While Lexi hadn't spoken up, I knew now that she would have if Katie hadn't. Von had no choice but to bring enough guards to protect us all. And I had to admit that I was comforted by the idea of keeping Dani where I could see her. Hopefully often. And naked.

"Yes!" Dani pumped her fist in the air and the other females smiled. All too easily their reaction pleased me.

Was this to be my fate; bending over backwards to please one human female?

I looked at Dani, at the sparkle and happiness in her blue eyes, and I realized that, yes, most likely, I was doomed.

"We will all be going once Von has secured the contingency of trusted guards."

While he'd agreed to the plan, I could tell from his tone

that he wasn't as eager as his mate. But from what we'd talked about, we had no choice. If Dani could escape this place and follow me to the capital, Lexi and Katie would, no doubt, accompany her. And the three of them roaming the world unprotected? Unacceptable.

I was grateful for his caution. Together, we could protect our mates, but I would feel better once Von brought the full contingent of Hunters he trusted, men who had no reason to betray me. I would complete the ascension, ensure the familial claim to the seat on the Seven, and assume my throne, so to speak.

And whoever had threatened my life? He would be found and eliminated.

"Thank you all." I meant it. Without their help, I had no idea where we would be now. And I was shocked at how quickly I had come to trust both Von and Bryn, Hunters I didn't know, but whose mates, with their happy smiles and glowing eyes, vouched for their standing as men of honor better than a dozen oaths of loyalty could have.

They all nodded and I heard Dani's stomach rumble.

She leaned up to murmur directly in my ear. "Someone made me hungry."

I stood, keeping her in my arms.

"Based on what you guys did last night, I'm surprised you lasted this long without tearing the kitchen apart." Katie's grin was accompanied by a wink as she stood and led the way to the kitchens. "There's a ton of food in here. Enough for a small army, which is good, since Von's bringing one."

In the kitchen, I placed Dani on her feet and watched, amused, as she sorted through the various items, piling food high on her plate before sitting at the large table.

I followed, filling my plate with the most nutritious offerings available, a mix of meat, fruit, bread and cheeses that would serve me well to replenish what I had lost in captivity and provide the maximum energy I would require for the rest of the afternoon with Dani naked and beneath me.

It would take Von several hours to return with the guards. Since we needed their additional protection to return to my home, there was nothing I could do except wait. Until then, Dani was all mine. Every perfect inch of her. And I was hungry for much more than food. My cock pulsed, elongated. I would take this time of peace, of quiet before the chaos of the ascension and the threat that still loomed, to focus on her. On showing her how much she meant to me. She was now a princess, but stripped bare, she was just my Marked Mate. Emphasis on *mine*.

"Eat, mate," I growled. "You will need your energy."

"For what?" She paused, a square of cheese and bread halfway to her lips. "Aren't we just lounging around until Von and Bryn get back?"

Allowing every lust-filled thought to show in my eyes, I shook my head. "Relaxing? No. Screaming? Perhaps. Clawing at the bed sheets? Begging me to taste you again? To sink my cock into that virgin ass?"

The food fell from her fingers onto her plate and she fumbled to retrieve them as Katie walked out of the room, a knowing smile on her face. Dani watched her go and turned to face me. "You are so bad."

"What? They know what we did, what we *will* do. Just be thankful I don't knock all of the food out of the way and take you here on the kitchen table."

Katie returned, reached her arm between us and set a

bottle on the table. "Here. You're going to need this. Have fun!"

She laughed as she walked off, leaving us alone.

Oil. She'd given us a bottle of oil, used for many things, including lubrication for ass fucking. I was liking her more and more.

"Gage!" Dani whispered, her cheeks a bright red. While she was so fierce, so passionate, there were moments like these where her innocence showed. It was endearing and charming.

Her mouth fell open as I met her pale gaze. Held it with my intensity.

"Eat. I will not have you lose energy halfway through the ravishment."

I watched the play of her throat as she swallowed. "Ravishment? Didn't you ravish me last night?"

I didn't respond. Instead, I ate, quickly and efficiently, handing her pieces of select meats and cheeses, those I knew to be as mild in taste as her Earthly palate. Based on the items she'd sampled then ignored, she had apparently not yet adjusted to Everian cuisine.

When she slowed, spending more time watching me than eating, I knew she was sated. At least her stomach was. As for her pussy, I knew it had to be wet based on the way she squirmed in her chair, the way her nipples were hard points beneath her borrowed shirt. She was as needy as me.

The time had come. Finally, I replied. "Yes. Ravishment." I cupped her jaw, ran my thumb over her lower lip. "Your first virginity became mine when you took me deep into your mouth, swallowed down every drop of my seed. It's time to claim your second sacred virginity; your hot, tight ass."

Her eyes darkened, her cheeks flushed and her pink tongue flicked out to lick the top of my thumb.

The memory of the taste of her skin, of her wet pussy, aroused me further. I could taste her still, her sweet juices lingering on my Hunter's tongue, even after our meal.

I never wanted her essence to fade from my senses.

To ensure that, I would taste her often. Fuck her. Fill her. For she was mine, and as soon as the official claiming was complete, by every law and custom of Everis, she would be mine forever.

I stood, grabbed the bottle of oil and held out my hand. "Come, mate. I will pleasure you until you beg me to stop." When she took my hand, I knew I had her consent, knew she wanted what would come next, would love it.

Smiling, she placed her hand in mine eagerly. "Promise?"

I groaned at the way she twisted my words into something carnal. "Yes, I promise you will come over and over." I pulled her close, holding her tightly, absorbing her sweet scent, her wild heat into my body. "Until you cannot remember any name but mine."

When I cradled her against my chest, she did not resist, but wrapped her arms around my neck and snuggled closer. The scent of her feminine arousal drifted to me, making me growl as I carried her back to our bed.

ani

GAGE LOWERED me carefully to the bed, then dropped the small bottle of lube beside me. I shifted to my knees, picked it up. The vial was glass and there was no label, but there was no doubt of its use.

Katie would have known. She'd been claimed. Everywhere. She would know how important the lube was. I clenched my bottom at the thought. I wanted Gage. Ached for him. My pussy was dripping just from his dirty talk in the kitchen.

But having that huge cock fill me...*there*...was a big step.

"I'm nervous," I admitted.

Gage was removing his shirt, but stopped mid-motion, then tugged it all the way off, dropped it to the floor.

"Are you afraid of me?" he asked.

I licked my lips as he opened his pants, let his big cock spring free. *He* was ready for the next step. Guys loved anal sex, right?

I lifted my gaze up from his cock, raking over his flat belly, the smattering of hair on his chest between his flat, cinnamon colored nipples, to the tendons in his neck, his strong jaw, full lips, then his dark, intense eyes. He was so powerful, so strong. He could hurt me. Snap me like a twig without even breaking a sweat. I was tiny in comparison to him.

"No. I'm not afraid of you."

He stepped close, reached out, stroked the backs of his knuckles down my cheek. I leaned into it, closed my eyes. "Then what is there to be nervous about?"

I laughed, looked up at him.

"You're big. Everywhere."

He grinned then and I knew I'd only inflated his big male ego. And the way his cock pulsed close to my belly, knew I'd inflated that, too.

"I just don't think I'm ready to take you yet. I'm small and well, the idea of you fucking my ass is hot and all, but my head's not into it."

He leaned down, kissed me. Gently, tenderly. "Ah, mate. It is my job to ensure you are ready, that you are begging for my cock to fill you. If you aren't begging, then I'm not doing it right."

I relaxed a little, glad to know he was taking charge, ensuring I was aroused enough and in the right headspace for the next claiming.

"First things first. I can't claim anything with all these clothes on."

I knelt before him and I helped him get Katie's borrowed clothes off me, lifting my arms to get out of the shirt, adjusting my legs to get the pants off. I was bare beneath; borrowing my friend's clothes didn't include underwear.

"I like you bare. I like knowing your pussy, those tart nipples are right there for me to touch, taste. Claim."

My skin heated from his words, from the look in his eyes as he took in my naked body. I wasn't used to such scrutiny, but I felt pretty. Beautiful, even. I knew he felt deeply for me. I sensed that when he held me close, caressed my skin with his hands, the brush of his lips. But this, the dark looks, the carnal promises of his words, made me feel needed. *Wanted*.

"Lay down. On your belly."

I frowned, but moved as he wanted. The softness of the sheet beneath me felt good, allowed me to relax. "I'm a virgin, but this doesn't seem like the right position to be in. Don't you need my butt up or something?"

Gage laughed before closing his eyes with a groan, as if I'd hurt him somehow. After a few moments when he seemed to have gathered himself, he grabbed the lube, opened it, poured a large amount into his hand, then dropped it back to the bed.

"We are going to have to do something about that delightful mouth of yours." He rubbed his palms together, then put his hands on my back, began to stroke up and down each side of my spine. Gently. Soothingly.

"Um, why are you rubbing lube all over me? Don't you put it on your cock?"

"Mate," he growled. "Silence. I only want to hear moans and cries and screams of pleasure. Or my name. Unless you tell me to stop, nothing else should come from those lips.

Close your eyes. Give your body over to me. Let the oil—not lube—sink into your skin."

Oil.

It did feel like oil, sleek and warm, allowing Gage's palms to slide easily over my muscles, working them. He was giving me a massage. Nothing more. I was naked, but his touch was not sexual. The promise of more was there, but he did nothing inappropriate. That was fine and all and I relaxed into his touch, into the way he settled my mind, made me forget my nerves.

But after a while, I wanted him to be inappropriate. My thoughts were solely focused on his palms, the way he used his fingers to work my muscles, to slide up and down my spine, over my ribs. The way he got close to touching the sides of my breasts since his hands were so big, but he never did.

I whimpered when he denied me that touch. My nipples, while pressed into the bed, were hard. Craved his touch. His play. And as he slid his hands down to the base of my spine, to the swell of my bottom, I parted my legs, hoping he'd take the hint and touch me there.

My pussy ached for his touch. His mouth.

I whimpered, shifted my hips.

"Need more, mate?" he asked. He hadn't spoken since he'd begun his massage, only shifting on the bed to position himself beside me.

"Your seduction plan is working. I'm not nervous anymore."

His hands didn't stop moving up and down my back. If his career as a prince fell through, he could always be a masseuse.

"Good. But you are not yet ready for my cock."

That was true. *Nothing* had touched me there and I doubted anyone's bottom went from zero to cock without a little revving of the engine.

His hands moved away. I watched as he drizzled more oil into his palms, rubbed them together again. Kneeling beside me, I couldn't miss the way his cock thrust out from his pants, but he did nothing about it. I assumed he'd opened them to alleviate the ache because it was big. A swollen cock like that couldn't fit in his pants comfortably.

The big head flared, a bead of fluid at the tip. I knew what that tasted like and my mouth watered for more.

"Not happening, mate. I see you looking at my cock, wanting it in your mouth."

"How did you—"

"You are my mate. I know you. You'll suck me dry and I want to come only when I'm nice and deep in your ass. I want to fill you with my seed. You'll come with me. I promise."

I squirmed at the truth behind his words. I wanted to come. I wanted to come with him inside me.

"Please," I whimpered.

Gage's hands settled on my bottom, kneaded the globes and his thumbs dipped inward, sliding over my pussy.

"Gage!" I cried. The touch was gentle. Hot. Wicked. And slick. My own arousal coated his thumbs, but the oil added to it, made his motions easy, the feel of it so incredible. And he wasn't even touching my clit. He was teasing me.

And it was working.

One hand worked its way up my back as the other slid over my pussy, cupped it, then brushed my clit just before a finger circled the entrance to my pussy. I pushed my bottom up, wanting him to go in. To fill me, even if it was just with a finger.

He retreated and I whimpered his name again.

"Beautiful, mate. But it's this hole I want now." His fingers migrated backward and brushed over my back entrance, the touch light, almost a whisper. His hand came away from my back and a second later, I felt a few drops of oil splash onto that virgin hole. A finger circled, worked the oil about.

"Wow," I said, the feel of him playing with me surprising. I had no idea I was so sensitive there, that it would be intense and pleasurable, the sensations pushing me higher, making my pussy clench deep. Hotter. Wetter.

Ignored.

I whimpered. And he hadn't even gone inside my ass. Just the damn circling.

"Gage!" I growled.

I heard him chuckle and I wanted to smack him, but was afraid his finger would move away. He was smiling down at me, his eyes filled with warmth and mirth.

"More?"

I nodded into the bed, closed my eyes.

"Good girl."

More oil fell and he worked it in, this time pressing more firmly. I resisted automatically, but he didn't stop. I didn't know how long he played there, giving my body time to adjust, to relax, to flower open for him. When I did, I groaned, the digit holding me open, filling me.

More oil followed, more sliding in and out, mimicking, I knew, what his cock was going to do soon enough.

There was some burning, the stretch odd, but it didn't

hurt. When he pushed deeper, then retreated, the slide of his finger made nerves flare to life.

I stiffened. "Oh my god."

Gage's other hand found my clit and I bent my knees automatically, spreading myself wide for him, giving him all the access he wanted.

One finger flicked and played with my clit, another worked into my bottom as he slid his thumb into my pussy. Played. Stretching me there as well.

The feel of it was so intense, so incredible, completely different than the feel of his mouth on me.

"I'm going to come," I warned.

"Good, mate. Come as much as you want."

I was lost by then, not interested in anything but the feel of what he was doing. And he was completely working my body, playing me like an instrument.

I came, my entire body tightening as a low moaning howl came from my throat. He pushed me through it, working his finger over my clit, inside my ass, my pussy, forcing me to ride one crest and leap on another.

My body wasn't sated, it was spinning out of control. Higher.

Within moments, I was on the edge again. Just as I was about to come, my fingers clenching the sheet, my body taut, he slipped his fingers from me.

"No!" I cried, almost in tears, needing the stimulation he provided.

But I shouldn't have worried. He wasn't going anywhere. Instead, he added a second finger to my ass, breaching me in one careful, slow press.

I came then on a scream, my hips pushed back so my

bottom stuck up in the air, his fingers going deeper as he continued to strum my clit.

My skin tingled, sweat bloomed over my skin. My brain sizzled, my thoughts completely fried.

"More," I panted. "I need more."

I did. It wasn't enough. It was like he was teasing me with his play.

"Shh," he crooned, trying to soothe me. "You're still not ready. Another finger to open you up. Another orgasm and then you'll be ready."

Another finger? Another orgasm? *Then* I'd be ready? By then, I'd be unconscious.

More oil was used, another finger added as I writhed and whimpered, moaned and begged. My clit was hard and swollen, my pussy dripping. I was so primed, so ready for him, I pushed up onto my forearms so I was on hands and knees.

"Now." I looked over my shoulder at him, gave him the look of death. "Fuck me *now*."

He grinned, but this time instead of being playful, it was tense. He'd been holding back, keeping all his need, his readiness to fuck me aside as he readied me. But my words, my vehemence behind them, must have been what he'd been waiting for.

He pulled away, shucked his pants and grabbed the oil, coating his cock liberally so it glistened with it. He knelt on the bed, settled behind me. I felt the flared heat at my prepared entrance, felt the press of it.

One of his hands came down by my head, and I felt his body along my back. His free hand cupped my breast, played with the nipple. My head came up, settled into the side of his neck.

"Please," I begged. I needed him inside me. I felt empty without him.

His hips pressed forward, the insistent push of his cock had me, at first, resisting, but then I exhaled, relaxed my muscles, and he popped in.

Gage growled and panted, holding still. I gasped, clenched, adjusting to him. He was so much bigger than his fingers.

After a moment, he pressed deeper, millimeters, then retreated. Again and again as I began to pant, began to adjust. In and out he moved until his hips bumped into my bottom, until I'd taken every thick inch of him.

He kissed my neck, bit the tender flesh where it met my shoulder. "Mine," he growled, then began to move.

He was fucking me now, slowly, steadily as his fingers pinched and plucked my nipples, his lips coasting over my shoulder.

I felt claimed. Pinned. Trapped and at the same time set free.

My mark burned. My body burned for Gage.

"I'm...I can't—"

"Come, mate, and I will follow. Mark you."

He pushed deep, a hard thrust as his hand dropped to my clit, my pussy, filling me up with his finger as he pushed deep.

I exploded.

There was no sound, only the milking of my inner walls wanting him deeper, keeping him there. In me, a part of me.

I wanted him to feel the pleasure he gave me, to share it with him.

I felt him swell, thicken, then his entire body go taut as

he growled, bit my shoulder and flooded me with his seed. Marking me. Coating me inside. Making me his.

Making him mine.

One more step until *he* was truly claimed. Until nothing could separate us.

Because the way I fell to the bed, his cock embedded deep, his body just off to the side of mine, the last thought I had before I fell into sleep was that I already was.

age

WE ARRIVED at the palace in the dead of night. It was agreed by Von, Bryn and myself along with the dozen Hunter guards Von brought, that the cover of darkness would keep my return a secret. At least until we were all safely within the walls and the guards could establish their protective perimeter. The existing palace guards, vigilant, as I expected, allowed Von's team onto the grounds on my orders and his men took control of my wing of the property. I informed them not to wake my mother or my sister, for a reunion at such a late hour was not necessary. Morning would be soon enough to deal with my sister's tears and my mother's theatrics.

And so I ensured Lexi, Katie and their mates had rooms of their own before I led Dani to mine. I refused to claim her final virginity. We were both too tired, and I wanted my mate wide awake when I took her sweet pussy. I would be on her for hours, making her come again and again. It was not the time.

Instead, she surprised me by dropping to her knees and taking my cock deep into her throat. While her motions were that of a novice, it was this innocence—and eagerness —that had me coming in hot spurts quickly down her throat. Loving the satisfied glean in her eye, I tossed her onto my large bed, pushed her thighs apart and worked her with my mouth and fingers until she cried out my name, over and over until she passed out. Only then did I tuck her into my arms and sleep.

With the light of day, my eagerness for my mate had not diminished. As Bryn had said, I doubted it ever would. Lying naked, wrapped around my soft, beautiful mate, I had no interest in ever leaving my rooms, let alone the bed. She was sound asleep, curled against my side with a contented smile on her face, even in slumber.

My chest filled with a pride I'd never felt before, knowing I'd made her happy, made her discover the pleasures of her body only I could give her. That she was safe and perfect and mine.

One more step, the final claiming, remained and my sated cock grew hard at the thought, even as the noise outside our bedchamber rose as the Hunters Von had brought with him from his team on Feris 5, the men he trusted with his mate's life, and mine, stood guard. From what I could hear, they were refusing entrance to the one person I was not excited to see.

Mauve.

Obviously, word of my return had spread through the palace and my respite was over.

Her shrill, demanding voice carried, as did the quieter platitudes of my sister somewhere behind her, trying to talk sense into the older woman. Patience had never been one of my mother's virtues. Nor obedience, and right now, Von was taking the brunt of it.

And not backing down.

My grin grew wider as he calmly told her to go sit and watch some comm vids and wait. *He* knew what we were doing in here, our need for privacy. I respected him more for his understanding that Dani and I needed to be together. Alone. It didn't matter that I'd been kidnapped and left for dead. I had my Marked Mate and nothing—not even my mother—was going to keep me from being with her. While I'd hoped to claim her final virginity this morning, it was not to be. The role of prince would have to take precedence. For now.

Next to me, Dani stirred, her blue eyes blinking slowly. When her gaze settled on me, the tenderness I saw was nearly my undoing. I couldn't stop myself; I leaned down and kissed her softly. Gently. With all the strange new emotions stirring to life in my heart.

I had expected the pairing between Marked Mates to be explosive, full of lust and desire. But I was wholly unprepared for the gentleness Dani was using to conquer me. I doubted she even knew she held such power.

"Hello, there," she whispered, holding my gaze. Her hand wrapped around my neck and she pulled me down for another kiss.

I didn't even try to resist. Why would I?

"Let me into that room this instant, or I'll give orders to

have you removed from this door and left to rot in the dungeon." Mauve's command reached Dani's ears and she pulled back, staring up at me with a bit of mischief in her eyes.

"I assume that's your mother?"

I grinned back. "In all her shrill glory."

Dani lifted her face, kissing me quickly, then shoved me away and burrowed under the covers. "You better go take care of that. I don't want to meet my future mother-in-law naked."

It wasn't my mother I was concerned about. It was more that I had no intention of allowing the other guards who would storm the room with my mother to see Dani in such a vulnerable state. She'd been fierce when she'd come to my rescue, strong. But with me, she allowed herself to be gentle. Weak. Submissive. That trust was not one I would betray, not in the smallest way. And that meant keeping everyone out of this bedroom.

"No one will disturb you, mate. Take your time. Come meet her when you are ready. The guards at the door will escort you."

She nodded, her eyes round with worry. "She's going to hate me, isn't she?"

I stroked my knuckles down her cheek, wishing the annoying woman in the hallway gone so I could settle beside Dani, hold her close and just...be.

"She will adore you." I leaned down and took my time kissing her, making sure she knew who she belonged to. "As I do."

She jumped when a loud pounding started on the door, followed by Von's voice. "You better get out here, Gage.

Before things get ugly." There was laughter in his voice, which did not please my mother.

"I *will* see my son. Now! You arrogant, elitist male, get the hell out of my way."

"Coming," I shouted out and Dani giggled when she heard my mother huff away from the door.

"About time. How long does that kind of thing take, big brother?" A laughing, feminine voice asked, and I glanced at Dani to see her cheeks turn pink in embarrassment, even though we hadn't even been doing any of the things Rayla teased about.

"Your sister?" she whispered.

"My sister," I murmured back.

"Oh, God." She rolled over and pulled the pillow over her head. "I'm never coming out of this room."

I laughed, climbed from the bed and prepared to face my family.

I went to my closet and pulled on the formal attire expected of the royal elite, those who served on the council of the Seven. I glanced longingly at the uniform I had borrowed from Bryn, the dark brown Hunter's jacket and pants piled on the floor where I'd let them fall the night before, feeling strangely saddened. Why was I suddenly annoyed at the lack of variety and choice in my wardrobe?

No. Not just my clothing. My education. My choice of mate. My future.

My life. It had all been laid out for me like a too-tight, formal suit. Since birth. And I'd been wearing it without complaint until the mark on my hand flared to life. Until Danielle saved not just my life, but my soul.

I opened the door, slipped out and quickly closed it

behind me, making sure to block my much shorter female family members from peeking around me. The Hunters knew better than to try to get a glance at my mate. They stood back a respectable distance, all except Von, whose back was to the door, his chest blocking my mother. He'd just recently found his own mate, claimed her in the planetary custom. He knew being interrupted was *not* what I wanted now, even if I was a prince and a member of the Seven.

Gripping him on the shoulder in thanks, I stepped out into the hallway. I glanced back at him, and he knew what I wanted before I spoke.

"No one will disturb her. You have my word."

"Thank you."

He nodded.

"I will greet you both, but not here in the hallway," I said to Rayla and Mauve. "I will not have my mate's rest disturbed."

I walked past my mother and sister to the family's private sitting area. I went barefoot, because I felt like it, and I knew the lack of decorum would irritate my mother.

The moment I stopped moving, Rayla threw herself into my arms. "Thank the gods, Gage! I thought you were dead."

She held me tightly, sobbing, as her mother stood stiff-lipped, her chin inclined. Mauve's gaze was cloudy, shadowed by obvious pain, but I doubted that pain was for me.

Rayla had always been Mother's pride and joy. Her most precious jewel. The most pampered and protected female in the capital. The surest way to distress my mother was to hurt Rayla.

I rubbed Rayla's back, my gaze searching the guards who

had accompanied them, knowing I would find one set of eyes locked on my sister.

Elon was there, his hand on his weapon, gaze darting to his mate, safe in my arms, to the other Hunters surrounding us. Von had brought twelve warriors to the palace and six of them surrounded me now. And my sister.

I held Elon's gaze, just long enough to let him know nothing would happen to her. He didn't know Von's warriors who stood beside him, but I trusted Von, and Elon would have to as well. Satisfied, his stance softened, but he continued to watch every move in the room, as did his two most trusted friends and fellow Hunters, Geoffrey and Thomar. For the first time, looking at Von and Bryn, I understood what that kind of brotherhood really meant. It was powerful, knowing I could walk away, and both Von and Bryn would die to protect what was mine. I would do no less for them, for my Danielle's friends, Lexi and Katie.

We would kill without hesitation. All of us. From an Elite Hunter, I expected nothing less.

His devotion to my sister was obvious. I recognized the look in his eyes. The possession. The hunger. My sister was his, and I respected that, because it was her choice as well. She'd told me as much when I told her I'd found my Marked Mate, before the attack that had nearly cost me my life. I said nothing, as I had no idea if she'd revealed her choice to Mother yet. It was not my place to say.

Based on the indulgent look the older woman gave us, I suspected my little sister had kept her love affair a secret.

With a sigh, we settled in the living area of my wing. Katie and Lexi appeared, settling in one of the chairs, Lexi on the center and Katie on the arm, after introductions were made. Bryn stood behind them, glaring at Mauve's men.

Obviously, they had not been part of the original plan. No one was to be trusted and having potential threats within arm's reach of his mate made the Hunter tense.

Von remained where I'd left him, guarding what was precious to me. Even without him, there was standing room only along the edges of the room as Von's warriors stood shoulder to shoulder with the palace guards that always accompanied my mother.

I informed them of what had happened to me, although I left out the gruesome details for the women's sakes. It wasn't something I wanted to recount anyway and was irrelevant. I had survived. That was the only thing that mattered now.

I spoke of Von and Bryn finding me, bringing me here, to a safe place. I did not say a word about Dani tracking me through our dreams, of her skills on a hunt. There had been no women Hunters in decades. But more than that, I didn't want the traitor, should he be in this room, to consider my mate a threat. If they wanted to assume she was meek, too weary from her mate claiming her to be present, then so be it.

"We should call an emergency meeting of the Seven," Mauve insisted. "Move up your ascension ceremony to tomorrow. We can't risk you again, Gage." She sat opposite me in a chair, her back ramrod straight, her bearing regal. As it always was.

Normally, I disagreed with her on most political issues. But in this, her reasoning was sound, if unreasonable. "Mother, the anniversary of father's death is two days away. You know, as well as I, that the other members of the Seven will not welcome such a breach in protocol."

"It's tradition, nothing more. There are no laws to forbid

it." Mother was not one to play by the rules: not if bending them benefited her family.

And the sooner I took my place on the council, the sooner I'd have full access to my father's power and contacts. I had been in an advisory role for the past year, attending meetings, not allowed to vote. But in two days, I would be fully recognized, as powerful as any other member of the Seven. A true force to be reckoned with, the entirety of Everian military warriors and Elite Hunters mine to command. I could even request assistance from the Coalition Fleet or their dangerous and powerful Intelligence Core.

At the moment, I was an enemy to be feared. After the ascension? I'd be a demon to those who threatened what was mine.

Our family wealth was substantial, but when surrounded by enemies, nothing was more helpful in protecting what was mine than powerful friends. "I agree. Two days was fine, but if it could be tomorrow instead, it would be better." I looked to Bryn. "Safer."

I met his gaze. If the ascension was moved up, any plans in place to do me harm during the ceremony could be impacted. He nodded.

She took a deep breath, and I watched her mentally make the calculations. "Yes. But it will not be a full coronation. We will have to host the ball at our home."

"A ball? Wonderful!" Rayla beamed. "I have a new blue dress, Gage. You must see it. It matches my eyes."

Rayla was so young, so innocent. So full of joy in the world. She was intelligent and well-educated, but not yet hardened by life. I wanted to keep her that way, and I glanced at Elon, hoping he would see to it.

"I'm sure you will look beautiful, as always. And having the ball at the palace will help with security. A smaller event. Easier to secure."

"Excellent." Mauve was grinning ear-to-ear now. "We'll use the coronation ball to announce your engagement! It will be perfect."

"Excuse me?" Dani's voice hit the room like a thunderclap and everyone went silent, swiveling to see who spoke.

My sister froze, her hand twisting in mine. My mother took her time, turning to inspect the woman I'd claimed as my own. Dani stood behind her, Von protectively at her back, blocking her from my mother's men. I owed him. A lot.

"Did you say engagement? But I thought..."

Her gaze darted to mine and I came to my feet instantly, going to her side. I pulled her into my arms, breathing her scent deeply into my lungs.

She was freshly showered, her damp hair curling at the ends to display her delicate face. She was so small next to me, much smaller than Mauve, and she wore borrowed clothing as well: Katie's soft black pants rolled up around her ankles. The shirt she wore was the one I'd tossed onto the floor when I took her. She was drenched in my scent, and I couldn't stop the feral pride that raced through me as she stood, barefoot, and stared down my mother.

"Danielle, my heart, this is Mauve, my mother." When neither one of them moved, I continued. "Mother, we talked of this before I left for the Touchstone. This is my Marked Mate, Danielle, from Earth. She came to Everis as an Interstellar Bride, from a planet called Earth. I told you of a Marked Mate the morning after our first dream share."

"Yes, but I thought...I mean, you said you never made it to the Touchstone. That you were kidnapped before you arrived. I just assumed—"

"She is my Marked Mate, Mother. Nothing, not even being kidnapped, could keep us apart."

"But you're a prince!"

"She's mine."

My mother scoffed, the sound making me want to break something. "But you belong to Everis, my son. She is from Earth. From what I've read, they are a new, very primitive culture barely admitted to the Coalition of Planets. The people will not accept her, Gage. You can not be mated to some—pardon me, dearest—" That was addressed to Danielle before she returned her gaze to me. "—some unknown commoner from an uncivilized world. Your desire for a Marked Mate is trumped by your duty to your people. Your responsibility to the Seven, to the stability of our planet, outweighs mere longing."

"Mother." It was the only warning I was going to give her.

"Keep her as your lover, Gage. Surely. Privately." Mauve finally held out her hand to Danielle, but not in welcome. More like a queen expecting a pauper to kiss her rings. "But you must marry someone worthy to be by your side." Her gaze returned to Danielle. "You know nothing of our ways, Danielle from Earth. Nothing of the duties and expectations of a princess."

I bristled at her words. The fact that she was ignoring the powerful bond I shared with my mate, throwing her alien origins in Dani's face made me see red. But I'd been schooled, my entire life, to remain calm. I held up my hand with the mark, palm out so my mother could see it.

Grabbing Dani's hand, I lifted hers, showed the mark, then held her hand so we were palm to palm. If that didn't get the fucking point across, I didn't know what would.

"My father may have married you out of duty, but I am not my father. He raised me to rule on the Sevens how I saw fit. Do what *I* thought was best for the planet. And while I would have agreed with you before my mark came awake, I can't now. The sacred lure of the mark is too pure, too strong. My need for Danielle is too powerful. Nothing, and I mean *nothing,* will separate us. Even my role as prince."

"I think it's wonderful," Rayla beamed at my mate, honest curiosity in her blue eyes. "I'm Rayla. I'm your new sister."

Dani's tentative smile was the only permission Rayla needed before rising and pulling my mate into a tight hug. I was thankful for her for breaking the tension. My mother was too uptight with the rules of the Seven. I had a feeling since she'd never found her Marked Mate, we would never see eye-to-eye. She would never understand.

"I'm so glad you're here! So happy for Gage. This is wonderful." Rayla pulled back, her smile even wider. "*You* are wonderful. Welcome to the family."

"Thank you."

8

I STEPPED BACK from Rayla's hug to find Gage at my back, felt his hand settled there. And I needed him touching me, keeping me grounded.

There was a whole lot of power flowing around the room. Too many Hunters. Too much family tension. I could feel it, though, and I was pretty damn sure Mommy Dearest wasn't going to join my fan club anytime soon. God, she was so passive aggressive, taking swipes at me left and right. Obviously, she believed my mind was as primitive as the planet I came from. I wasn't *worthy* of her precious son.

Gage wrapped his arms around my waist and I leaned back, happy to be in his arms while facing the proverbial firing squad. Everyone in the room was studying me—especially Mauve—and I felt not just underdressed, but like an ugly insect pinned down and being fried with a beam of sunlight focused through a magnifying glass.

Maybe I was being paranoid, but I felt like an outsider. Unwelcome and unwanted. And Mauve's guards? They were just doing their job, protecting their charge from a possible threat. Me.

Gage was different. Maybe Lexi and Katie, too, but they were also from primitive Earth. The undercurrent of tension was because Gage was with *me*.

For him, I'd endure. I didn't feel any tension from him. Did he even notice how uncomfortable this whole meet-and-greet was? Or was this normal for him?

"We will use the coronation ball to announce that I have found and fully claimed my Marked Mate. That will turn the tide of public interest away from the kidnapping, and perhaps, give us time to discover who was behind the attack." Gage's comment wasn't really one at all, it was a command, and everyone in the room knew it.

"Very well." His mother inclined her head to me, but there was no warmth in her eyes. It was as if a cold breeze had blown through an open window.

I suddenly felt sorry for my mate. His sister was warm and friendly, but whoa. His mother was a regular viper. And she had her sights set on me. "Welcome to the family, Danielle."

Oh yes, I was so *not* welcome. The witch.

But then, he *had* warned me about her.

"Thank you." Whatever. Gage was mine and we were one virginity away from making it completely and totally official. Not that having Gage's cock in my pussy was going to change anything between us now. The mark proved a bond much deeper than the ridiculous claiming custom.

Oh, I wanted Gage's cock in my pussy, fucking me hard and deep. I squeezed my thighs together at the thought, but I didn't feel the need to do it just so some archaic rule could be met. I just wanted him. Every way I could have him. Since Mauve probably wouldn't appreciate that sentiment and dislike me all the more for corrupting her son with my primitive sexual needs, I said nothing. Instead, I smiled at her, a real smile, with just one thought running on repeat in my head. *I win. I win. I win.*

Gage seemed oblivious, but when I turned my head to Katie and Lexi, their raised brows and subtle roll of the eyes let me know they were with me. They saw it. Felt the...freeze from Mauve. God, it was nice to have friends. Real friends.

"Until we find the traitor who tried to kill me, Von, Bryn and his men will be in charge of my personal security." Gage angled his head toward Bryn, sure of the Hunter and the plan.

"Don't you think that's a bit extreme?" Mauve asked. "We don't know these men. We can't let strangers into our home."

Yet she was amongst them now. She had some serious balls to insinuate they were a threat while she was a guest in her son's home, under his protection.

"I know them." I spoke up and stepped away from Gage's warmth. If this woman and I were going to do this dance for the rest of our lives, I wasn't going to let her think I was an easy target. Better for her to learn now how things were going to go. She was no longer the female in Gage's life. While Gage didn't think that at all, it was obvious she did.

"I trust Von and Bryn," I said. "I don't trust your men. They allowed your son to be taken out from under your nose. My friends won't."

Mauve's nostrils flared and the stick up her ass went a tad deeper. Yeah, she was never going to like me.

All of Von's men weren't, technically, *my* friends, but they all puffed out their chests and straightened their shoulders, so I figured they didn't mind being claimed by a future princess.

Shaking her head in resignation, Mauve rose. "Very well, if you think this is best. I have work to do to move the ascension and the ball."

What a spiteful, little—Gage's hand settled on my shoulder. The touch instantly soothed me, for now. I *hated* passive aggressiveness. I much preferred aggressive-aggressive.

She left, all but three of her guards trailing after her. I recognized the men from the news feed earlier. One was the man Gage had pointed out as Rayla's chosen mate. Elon. He and two others were glued in place, waiting for Rayla to accompany them. They were Rayla's guards. Her protection.

Rayla, however, wasn't in a hurry. The moment the door closed behind Mauve and her guards, Rayla let out a huge sigh. All the tension left the room with the evil step-monster. Gage laughed. "I see she hasn't changed."

How was he laughing? Was he used to her? Did he not see she hated my guts?

"Never," Rayla commented. She held out her hand and Elon walked to her side, such love and tenderness in his eyes that I had to look away. Did Gage look at me like that? "Big brother, I'd like you to meet Elon."

Gage smiled and held out his hand. "An honor."

Elon took Gage's hand and bowed slightly. "The honor is mine that Rayla chose me."

"Agreed," Gage replied. "But she has, and I trust you will honor and protect her as a true mate should."

"Always," Elon insisted, his arm going around her waist.

"Do we have your blessing, Gage?" she asked, her eyes alight with hope. "Officially? I want to announce our mating at the coronation ball." Rayla's gaze darted from Gage to me, a touch of worry showing. "If that's all right with you, Danielle? I don't want to take anything away from you."

Rayla was everything her mother was not, and I knew we were going to be great friends. "Please, both of you, call me Dani. And I can't *wait* to see the look on your mother's face when you do."

Gage

I'D NEVER WANTED to be a prince less in my life. Every other Hunter on the planet who'd found their Marked Mate didn't have their focus divided between her and the duties of being one of the Seven. The complicated, archaic formality to officially become my father's successor; I had an ascension ceremony. No, I *was* the ascension. Without me, it wouldn't happen. There would be no reason for it.

There was someone who wanted me dead, who'd gone to great lengths to make that happen, and he'd almost succeeded. He just hadn't taken Dani's innate Hunter skills that saved me into account. Thank fuck.

I sighed. If that wasn't enough, I had a mother who wanted me to mate my stepsister, even after introducing both of them to my Marked Mate. It wasn't as if I'd dragged some random Everian female off the street to claim. Dani was my fucking *Marked Mate.* How many times did I have to tell Mauve that? Prove it to her?

None. No more. I didn't give a shit what Mauve thought. The ascension ceremony would happen tomorrow. I had guards, loyal to me, keeping me and Dani safe. Friends, too, in Bryn and Von. They knew to watch all our backs.

I had everything I wanted, except Dani beneath me, my cock buried deep in her tight pussy. I wanted that last virginity, wanted to claim it, and her, as mine forever. I wanted no one, nothing to separate us. To prove to the entire planet that she was my love.

"Is there anything else you need?" I all but growled, impatient, frustrated and horny as hell.

I looked to Bryn and Von. In a day, I'd laid my life—and Dani's—in their hands. Therefore, they were the closest and my most trusted advisors. More so than the other members of the Seven, of the royal guard. Of even my family.

"Not at this time," Von replied. "We've continued the search. My best Hunters—"

"He means me," said Bryn.

Katie laughed but Von ignored him completely. "My best Hunters, one of whom is Bryn, have not been able to uncover any new leads, Gage. Whoever betrayed you seems to have disappeared without a trace."

"Sounds like one of us," Elon commented, and I turned to him and the two Hunters who were often at his side, Geoffrey and Thomar. I had known them for years, Geoffrey having served my father before his death. They were good men. Trusted men. Obviously, Elon felt the same, for he had his beloved, my sister, under their protection.

"Yes, I agree," I replied with a decisive nod. "Which

means our enemy is well trained and extremely dangerous. I am trusting you will see to Rayla." I didn't form the words as a question, for it wasn't one. He'd said he'd protect my sister with his life and I believed him. Believed the affection between them. Now, I just wanted them gone. Safe, but elsewhere.

Elon nodded, took the hint and led Rayla away, Geoffrey and Thomar turning and following on their heels, their gazes ever watchful.

I glanced about at those who remained. "If no one needs us, then my mate and I will be in our quarters. We don't wish to be disturbed."

"But she needs a dress!" Katie all but shouted. Bryn wrapped an arm about her, keeping her from coming our way.

"Love, let them be," he murmured in her ear. She sagged against him and angled her head so he could kiss her neck.

"But they need—" she began.

"Privacy," he clarified.

"Oh!" Katie said, a smile spreading across her face. "Right. The dress can totally wait."

I watched as Dani blushed, realizing my intent. Yes, my intent was to get her naked, wildly aroused and claimed. No one better dare stand in my way. I doubted my balls would survive.

"Have fun!" Lexi said, giving a little finger wave and winking.

While Dani was slightly mortified, I was far from it. I had a task to accomplish and my cock was in complete agreement. In fact, my cock was the brain making the decisions right about now.

I took Dani's hand and led her out of the room. "Come,

mate. Let's get behind a locked door before anyone else needs me for something. The only thing I need to do now is get my cock into your pussy, stretch it open and mold it just for me."

My pace quickened with the need to do just that.

"Gage," Dani said, a little breathlessly.

"What?" I asked, my focus down the hall, my stride long and quick.

"You're going too fast. I can't keep up."

I was practically running. "I am eager. And worried someone will come up with something else to keep me from my task."

"Yes, but your haste is hurting my ankle," she said.

I stopped abruptly and she bumped into my side. I spun about, my hands going to her shoulders, and I bent at the waist to look at her. I saw the wild, wide eyes, the pinch of pain about her lips. "What's wrong with your ankle?"

"It's my bad ankle," she replied, as if that explained everything.

"We healed it with the ReGen wand," I replied. I glanced down her body, but couldn't see anything wrong because of her pants being in the way.

"You eased the swelling, yes. But it's never going to be fully healed."

I frowned. "What the hell do you mean 'never fully healed'? Of course, it's healed."

She sighed. "Some wounds aren't fixable and you have to live with them. I've lived with this for a while. It's better since the surgery, but I pushed it too hard tracking you. I'm glad I did, don't get me wrong. I just have to favor it for a few weeks until the swelling stops and the tightness lessens. But can you slow down?"

I stood to my full height. "Are you telling me you have been injured all this time and didn't tell me?"

"Well...yes." She shrugged with a nonchalance that pissed me off. "I'm used to it."

"I'm not," I countered. Horrified. "I won't have you injured without telling me. I won't have you hurting. Walking quickly should not be something you can't do. I won't allow it."

She burst out laughing. "You won't *allow* it? This isn't something you can decree and be fixed just because you're a prince." She snapped her fingers.

I pressed a button on the comms unit on my wrist as I eyed my mate. "This is your prince. I am bringing my mate to the med center now. She has an *injured ankle* and it needs to be repaired immediately."

"You're mad," she replied when I signed off. Her hands moved to her slender waist and she tapped her shoe on the floor.

I ran my hands through my hair. "Mate, I'm furious with you for keeping your pain a secret. Your burdens are mine. You must give them to me and I will fix them."

"How are you going to fix this?"

"By taking you to the doctor. Most likely you will spend time in a ReGen pod."

"But you have an ascension ceremony and a ball. I can't be in the hospital with a bum ankle. And what the hell is a ReGen pod?"

Von and Bryn came down the hallway. "Why are you two out here arguing instead of in there fucking?" Bryn asked, pointing toward the door to my quarters.

I groaned. "My mate has an injured ankle."

"From walking down the hall?" Von added.

Dani rolled her eyes at the men. "No, it's from a wilderness trip in Montana. I was hiking in the backcountry with a group from Cincinnati and a rock gave out beneath me as I was crossing a stream. I rolled it and one of the bones snapped."

"It was treated with primitive Earth medicine and needs to be healed," I explained. I had no idea where Montana was or if Cincinnati was a country or a region or a mountaintop and I doubted the other two did either. But that wasn't the point. She'd been injured on Earth and treated by Earth medicine.

"I told you,"—she began, her words coming out through gritted teeth—"it's as good as it's going to be. You just need to slow down."

Von and Bryn's eyebrows were up beneath their hair, then they grinned. Von even slapped me on the shoulder. "Gage, sir, welcome to the club. You join Bryn and I in the Hunters who have stubborn Earth women as mates."

I was not amused and I narrowed my eyes at them. Stubborn, yes, but their mates were fully claimed, their cocks satisfied. Their mates knew well and truly who they belonged to. Dani was not mine, not yet. Someone could challenge our match. Danielle, my beautiful, stubborn female, could change her mind. I needed to claim her; the primitive demand roaring through my Hunter's blood with a fury I'd never felt before, not even on a hunt. But she was injured. Her health came first. She was mine to care for, and I would not allow her to hobble in pain when it was unnecessary and barbaric. "We are going to the med center at once."

"I can't be laid up for days," Dani repeated. "Are you trying to get rid of me?"

I sighed. "I'm trying to make you well so I can fuck you unconscious. And as for days, you will be healed within two hours."

"Two hours?" she asked, sounding as if she found that unbelievable.

"Yes, two hours that I would rather spend in bed with you. But I will not claim you knowing you are injured."

She grabbed my arm, gripped it tightly, looked up at me with eyes as desperate to fuck as I felt. "Claim me. Seriously, Gage. I'm fine. My stupid ankle is *fine.* I've been walking on it for months. I had surgery. A cast. Crutches. And I don't need my ankle to...you know." Her blush was charming but did not sway me. "Gage, we can go to the doctor later. *After.*"

"You will go now," I said, my tone serious, even though my cock ached to fill her. Her arguments were not helping my growing anger at her inept Earth healers. Surgery? A cast? What in the name of the gods was a cast? "I will not have you in pain, mate. There will be no arguments, or I will place you over my knee and spank you like a disobedient child."

"I'll *be* in pain if you don't claim me. If you don't touch—"

I couldn't let her finish the thought or I'd give in to her demands. I also had no interest in arguing further, especially in a fight I was absolutely going to win in the end. I leaned down and tossed her over my shoulder, Von and Bryn stepping out of the way. "Two hours, Hunters. Two hours and I will bring my mate back and then we will be in our quarters. Undisturbed."

I heard their laughter as I carried my angry mate to the med center, the heated scent of her arousal making me growl and pick up my pace.

9

"I'm nervous," I admitted. I was sitting on an exam table in the medical center. Gage had helped me change out of my clothes and into what looked like middle school gym clothes. A mint green t-shirt and a pair of loose similarly colored shorts. Gage had argued with a tech and refused a gown, stating that the princess needed more modest garb than that. The tech had argued pants wouldn't work because it covered her ankle and they'd compromised on shorts.

Fortunately, that had distracted me, but only for a time.

I didn't like doctors' offices. Hospitals. Who did? It was very similar to an ER on Earth, but the gadgets and lights on the walls were more *Star Trek* than County General. It was sterile, white and chilly. But Gage stood beside me and ran his knuckles down my cheek. I wasn't cold.

"The last time you said that, I made you come before I

slid my cock into that gorgeous ass and claimed it. Do you want me to slip my hand into your pants and get you off before the doctor returns?"

I was equal parts turned on and petrified. I couldn't help but squirm on the table, and the way his pants were tented told me he was as affected as me. I knew he was trying to distract me, but was also quite serious. If I needed to come to relax, he wouldn't hesitate to make that happen.

"We can still come back," I offered. "We don't have to do this now. I've lived with my ankle this way for a while now."

"And you have lived this long without being fucked. And both things will be resolved today. You are my mate and I will see to *both*."

As if being his mate cleared it all up. While I was pleased he felt so deeply for my well-being, I was also very perturbed. I wanted sex. Now. Finally, finally we were going to do it and then my stupid ankle was what cock blocked him. Ridiculous. But nothing I said or did would sway him. So, I gave up. It didn't mean I wasn't scared of the unknown. Kind of like getting your wisdom teeth pulled. You had an idea of what it would be like, but it didn't matter until it was your turn to have pliers in your mouth.

"I'm not familiar with your technology," I said. "I know what a ReGen wand is; but what is a ReGen pod?"

"It's a statis bed that allows your body to regenerate, to heal in ways it can't while you are awake," the doctor said, coming into the room. He held a tablet similar to what Warden Egara used back at the Brides Program Testing Center.

We turned to look at the Everian and he offered both of us a slight bow. I was unused to being shown such deference, but I doubted my mate, *the prince*, had the same problem. The doctor was big, like Gage, but was perhaps a decade older. While he had a serious demeanor, his voice was calm.

"You're going to put me to sleep?" I gripped Gage's hand. Hard. I wasn't thrilled with being put to sleep so they could do things to me I didn't understand.

"Before that, we will operate on your ankle."

"Operate?" Gage asked. "That's drastic. Whatever for?"

The doctor's expression didn't change, even with Gage's cranky tone. That didn't make me feel any better, knowing an operation was something even my mate didn't want—and he wanted me healed pronto.

"She has pins in her ankle bones holding them together. A low-quality metal not found anywhere on Everis, except in your mate's ankle. The ReGen pod can't do its job with the metal inside her. We will remove it, then the pod will complete the healing."

"I can't have surgery now," I countered. "You've got your ascension ceremony tomorrow. The ball. I've told you, we'll wait because I don't want to miss it. The ankle isn't a big deal."

Gage gave me a look that had me biting my lower lip. It was going to be done whether I wanted it or not.

"How long will this take?" Gage asked the doctor.

"Three hours."

"Three hours?" I asked incredulously. "That's it?"

"This is Everis, Princess." I was not used to being addressed as princess and it felt...weird. "It would be shorter, but I must remove the metal first."

I looked up at Gage. "I'm not nervous now. I'm scared."

"I won't leave your side," he reassured.

"You can't stay with me in the operating room," I countered, not thrilled.

"I won't leave your side," he repeated, but was eyeing the doctor as he said so.

"That is correct. He may remain. I can give you a blocker for the metal removal if you wish to remain conscious. I advise that you are sedated instead because there really is no need to cause yourself any kind of mental trauma witnessing metal being pulled from your flesh. However, it is your choice."

When he put it that way... I shivered at the thought of watching my ankle be sliced open and him tugging out the pins, pain blocker or not.

"After that is complete, you will be moved to the ReGen pod for two hours. There, you will be unconscious to let the machine do its work, but the prince may remain at your side for that. For all of it."

Gage squeezed my hand this time. "Doctor, will you give us a moment while you get ready?"

It was happening whether I wanted it or not. And right now. I knew Gage wouldn't let me leave the med center until this was resolved.

"Certainly."

He left the room with another bow and Gage sat down on the exam table beside me. He lifted me—with ridiculous ease—onto his lap, stroked my hair. He felt warm, his body hard, but he had a gentle nature. At least with me.

"If I argue with you, tell you I don't want this, you'll probably have me sedated, won't you?"

He was a bossy alpha male, so I had an idea of his response.

"Just think. In three hours, your ankle will be

completely healed," he said instead of answering. "No primitive metal. No swelling. You may run as much as you wish. And I promise, I will chase you." He kissed the top of my head.

I didn't say anything, just savored the feel of his hold, of his hand as it soothed me, sliding up and down my back.

The doctor returned. "Do you wish for a pain blocker while I perform the surgery or do you wish to be sedated?" he asked me. Fortunately, he knew better than to ask my mate.

I looked up at Gage. He was so close, if he tilted his head down an inch, our lips would touch. "Can you hold me while they put me to sleep?" I asked, biting my lip. I was really nervous, my heart pounding. Normally, blood didn't bother me much, but when it was mine? I was going to pass out.

Gage did kiss me then, gently. Sweetly.

"I will hold you, and I will not let go of your hand the entire time. I promise."

I looked to the doctor. Sighed. "All right. Put me to sleep."

The doctor moved about the room as Gage began to murmur in my ear. Soft words, just for me. "In three hours, when you awaken, we will go back to our quarters and I will strip you bare."

The doctor returned and I expected him to have an IV or a shot of some kind. He had a wand that looked like the ReGen one we'd used in the shuttle that had healed Gage's cuts and bruises, the swelling in my ankle.

"I love your breasts and sucking on your pink nipples. I love your taste; your sweet honey is all for me."

If the doctor heard Gage's carnal words, he made no sign

of it. He fiddled with a few buttons on the wand as my mate continued to whisper to me.

"When you are beneath me in three hours, I will slide my cock into your pussy. I will claim your last virginity you've saved just for me."

The doctor lifted the wand and a red light came on. He waved it in front of my face and I couldn't help but follow it with my eyes. I relaxed into Gage, wilted and felt sleep tug at me. My eyes closed and I sank into Gage's voice.

"You'll be so wet, so tight, I will lose my mind. *You* make me lose my mind. My mate, my lo—"

Gage

THE DOCTOR OVERESTIMATED the time for Dani to heal by twelve minutes. Thankfully. I sat and waited for the clear lid of the ReGen pod to open so I could reach in and hold her hand once again. I'd held it as the doctor cut her ankle open, retrieved the small bits of Earth metal and placed her in a ReGen pod. But the pod required the lid to be closed to work, and so I'd sat beside it, watched and waited as the flesh knit and healed. I monitored the timer until it ran out, felt the vibrations and hum of the unit cease. The lid slid open and I could once again touch her, hold her hand. I'd promised and I'd kept it as best I could, considering medical intervention.

Then I held my breath waiting for her to wake.

My love. My heart.

She'd come across the galaxy to save my life. And if she

wanted me to do something as simple as hold her hand, I would.

And wait with the impatience of a male in need of his mate whole and healthy. To see her pale eyes alight with happiness, arousal. To see her smile and know it was all for me.

When her fingers finally twitched, then clenched mine, I knew she was coming awake. Within a minute, she blinked. Then again. I knew the second she focused on me, that she was truly with me again.

Three hours was too long. I trusted in Everian medical technologies, but that didn't mean I wouldn't worry, even after the doctor assured me everything was fine. With Dani's vivacious spirit and her willingness to take reckless chances, I knew I'd be worrying about her the rest of my life.

She popped upright in the ReGen pod so fast she almost whacked my chin. I laughed, sitting back, then stroking her hair back from her face. Her cheeks had color and she was alert, as if she'd just taken a nap instead of had an operation and ReGen time.

"Am I...is it all better?" she asked, her voice hoarse. I picked up a cup of water, held it out for her. She took it from me, drank greedily. I wiped the drop that clung to her lower lip with my thumb.

The doctor came into the room then. "My tablet said you were awake." He smiled at both of us. "Let's test that ankle, shall we?"

He looked to me, knowing I wouldn't let him touch her, not now that she was well. I stood, scooped her up and set her on her feet, but kept an arm about her waist. The pale green shorts and shirt were large on her, reminding me just how small, how fragile she was.

She shifted her weight from foot to foot, wiggled and twisted her ankle from side to side. The doctor grabbed a ReGen wand and another sensor and went down onto one knee before her.

"Lift your leg."

With my arm about her, she was able to maintain her balance and follow his instructions as he did various scans.

"It doesn't look any different," she said, her head tipped down, watching him.

"The operation was to remove the metal," he commented, looking at his implements' readings. "The ReGen pod healed the bone and the cuts I made to get the metal out. But the scars from your surgery on Earth will remain. Jump up and down."

I loosened my hold, held my breath once again as she followed the doctor's order, coming off the ground a few inches. I saw the way her breasts bounced, even beneath the loose shirt and I was glad the doctor's gaze was focused much lower.

"It feels...fine," she said hesitantly. She looked to the doctor, then to me. Hope shined.

"The scans test normal. Skipping the complex clinical terms, the ankle is healed. All prior damage is gone."

"That's it?" she asked, marveled.

The doctor stood. Smiled. "That's it." He looked to me, said, "No restrictions."

My cock swelled at his inference, at the knowledge Dani was well, whole and nothing was stopping me from finally —FINALLY—claiming her.

"Thank you, Doctor."

The man offered another slight bow. "I am honored to serve."

When he left, I tipped Dani's chin up, kissed her, just a swipe of my lips across hers. She lifted up onto her tiptoes, flung her arms about my neck. I lifted her so her feet cleared the floor, cupped the firm globes of her ass and she wrapped her legs about my waist. Her small breasts pillowed against my chest, her nipples hard points.

"Gage," she breathed, taking the kiss deeper.

The rigid length of my cock was nestled against her pussy, only our clothes in the way.

"Now...please," she begged.

I pulled my head back, but didn't put her down. "Not here."

She shook her head. "No. Not here. But now. Please. I want to be yours, in every way. You promised."

I groaned, my cock pulsing, pre-cum escaping.

We'd had so many setbacks. Kidnapping. Meddling family. Injuries. Claiming Dani was not an easy task to accomplish, but now was the time. It *was* going to happen. I just had to get her to my quarters and lock the door. The ascension ceremony was tomorrow and I wanted my mate, fully claimed, by my side. Until then, neither of us was needed.

Dani wiggled in my hold and I lowered her to the floor. Pushing out of my arms, she walked around the room, hopped up and down. Her breasts bounced beneath the plain shirt once again. The garment and matching green shorts were unisex and unattractive, but my balls ached with the need to fill her. She could wear a sack and I would find her appealing.

"Mate," I growled, my fingers itching to slip beneath the shirt and cup her breasts, to play with her sensitive nipples.

She looked up at me through pale lashes. "Yes?" she replied coyly.

"I watched them cut open your ankle, pull out pieces of metal. While I believe you are well, I do not wish to cause you harm."

"I'm fine," she said, laughing, clearly impressed by Everian technology. "Amazingly, I am. Completely healed."

"If you aren't, then I will toss you over my knee and spank you."

Her cheeks turned pink and her eyes flared with need. She bit her lip. "You'll have to catch me first."

And she was off, dashing out of the room.

Oh, she was in for it now. A spanking and a sound, thorough fucking were happening.

10

"I THOUGHT you said you were spanking my ass for arguing with you," I said, my voice soft. I was naked in the bathing tube—which mere mortals called a shower—with Gage— and he was washing me, running his soapy hands over every inch of my body. No part of me was left untouched. Unlike the tubes at the Touchstone and at Bryn's home, this one was large, easily big enough for two.

"You will learn, mate, that when it comes to your health and safety, I will not tolerate disobedience. You are surrounded by Elite Hunters, Dani, men strong enough to snap your delicate neck with barely a thought. And we have enemies. Never argue with me. I can't tolerate seeing you in pain, love. I can't. Don't ask it of me." He didn't look me in the eye as his hands gently roamed my body, assuring himself I was healed. Whole. Ready for him.

Catching his hand on my hip, I lifted it to my lips and kissed him. God, how the hell had I gotten so lucky? Tears gathered, burning the back of my eyelids as I dropped his hand back into the water and turned my head to wipe them away. Crying was stupid. This wasn't me.

And I wasn't a Marked Mate, either. I didn't have alien—Everian—ancestors. And I wasn't going to officially become a princess tomorrow either.

Right. Somehow my plans for my life had gone *way* off track. Not that I was complaining.

Somehow, Gage knew exactly what I needed. While the surgery and healing in the ReGen pod had felt like a blink of an eye, I still felt as if I'd spent time in a hospital. I saw the dark look in his eyes, felt his need in every taut muscle of his body, heard the deep timbre of his voice. Knew he needed to touch me, assure himself that I was well and healed and his. He wanted me as much as I did him.

While he could easily clear my mind of all thought with a few kisses, I wanted to be clean, to wash the time in the med center from my body. I wanted to clean that time from Gage's mind, too. I knew he'd been there, witnessed the surgery, the cutting and the blood. I knew the ache I'd felt finding him in that cave, beaten and bleeding. Really knowing him, knowing his touch and his smile and his heart would have made it ten times worse.

And as protective and possessive as these Everian Hunters seemed to be, I could only imagine the hell he'd gone through watching me bleed while he was helpless to do anything about it. That had to have been pretty intense. He needed to touch me, to feel every inch of me, to know I truly was whole before he took me to his bed. I had a feeling he'd be gentle this first time—I assumed—but I didn't want him to hold back. Not for a reason as silly as a months old ankle injury.

Besides, what injury? Ha! Those ReGen pod things were some kind of miracle.

My ankle felt different. It didn't ache, didn't feel weak. The tightness, the stiffness that had lingered for months, was gone and I knew the doctor's scans were accurate. I was fine. I'd have the scars from Earth to remind me of what had happened, but I didn't care. Scars proved people lived and mine were the only outward sign that I'd ever been on Earth. It would be my reminder of the life I left behind. The wound, now healed, would remind me of how far I'd come. I had scars on the outside, but inside? My ankle was perfect now. Whole. Just like the rest of me.

"Once I get you to our bed, I'm not letting you up until tomorrow." His hands roamed, slick with suds, over my belly to rise and cup my breasts as the hot water poured over both of us.

My head fell back, my eyes closed as he walked me backward, until my back hit the colder surface of the ceramic wall. "I think that part of me is clean," I murmured after what felt like minutes of his fingers playing with my sensitive nipples.

I felt him drop to his knees before me. "Then I shall move on to other places."

Other places just happened to be between my thighs. His hands moved lower to lift one of my legs up and over his shoulder, opening me to him. He didn't delay; perhaps he'd been delayed for far too long. His mouth found my very center, the flat of his tongue running up and over me with such skill and precision I cried out. My hand slapped against the wall of the tube for balance, even though I knew he wouldn't let me fall.

"Gage!" I cried. Heat pulsed through my veins, just from the slick caress of his talented tongue.

"Yes, mate?" he teased.

I opened my eyes, looked down at my mate, naked and kneeling. He was so handsome, so perfectly mine. Seeing him there, between my legs, devouring my pussy like a man possessed was possibly the hottest thing I'd ever seen in my life.

"This pussy is mine." He nipped at my thigh as he slid two fingers inside me, slowly opening me up, stretching me for his much larger cock. There was a small sting, a bite of pain, but when he broke that barrier, he groaned. "Mine. Fucking mine."

His mouth closed over my clit as he slowly, carefully, fucked me with his fingers. His tongue was far from gentle, sucking, flicking. Tasting.

Owning me. I was spiraling high, the new sensations strong, but not enough. I wanted him inside me, his body pressed to mine. I wanted to be covered with his heat. Enveloped. Overwhelmed. I wanted to let go.

"Please." I was begging. I didn't care.

He pulled out of my pussy, circled my opening, pushed deep as his tongue worked miracles.

I came, my body collapsing against the wall of the tube, only his hand, his mouth, his bulk holding me in place as my pussy rippled around his fingers.

When I could speak, I reached down, cupped his face. Met his dark eyes. God, I was hot, my pussy still pulsing in aftershocks I knew he could feel. He looked at me, but he fucked me with his fingers. Slow. Sensual. So very wicked.

I felt wicked. And I knew what I wanted. Something new. Something naughty and wild and so unlike me that I almost didn't tell him what I wanted, what I needed.

"Dani, I can see it in your eyes. Tell me. Tell me what you want."

When he looked at me like that, I could not deny him. Or myself. "Spank me."

Heat flared as he wiped his mouth with the back of his hand. He stood, wrapped his arms about me and lifted me out of the tube. The water shut off automatically as he grabbed a towel, dried me from head to toe. The friction only made me hotter, needier. Then he quickly dried himself before tossing the towel aside, angling his head.

"Bed. Now." He was perfect. Magnificent. Hard slabs of muscle, broad shoulders, narrow waist, thrusting cock, fluid pearling at the tip. He was all mine. Every delicious inch of him.

I bit my lip to keep from smiling as I walked into the bedroom. I heard him follow and I went to the bed, looked over my shoulder at him, knew he was watching my every move.

I knew the ReGen pod had healed my ankle, but I felt rejuvenated. As if I'd had the best night's sleep *ever*. It made me...bold. While I was hot for Gage, I didn't know exactly what was coming next. He did. And that made me want to tease him. To make him crazy, well, for me.

I leaned forward, put my hands on the bed, my bottom out. He'd already claimed me there, the most intimate of acts, so I shouldn't feel modest.

I didn't. The opposite, in fact.

"Like this?" I wiggled my bottom, knew he could see

everything. My wet pussy—I was so wet my thighs were slick with it—and my breasts thrust out beneath me.

"Mate, you are being *very* naughty," he commented, striding toward me, his cock thrust out, aiming straight for me.

And he liked me naughty. The turn of his lip, the way his eyes darkened impossibly further as he eyed me in my provocative position. My pussy in the air and on display. It was a deliberate taunt, a temptation I did not want him to resist.

I wanted him to be mine. All mine. Officially. Legally. Every way I could claim him. I wanted his seed inside me. His child in my womb. His cock? His body? His mind? His heart? His soul? His seed?

Mine.

I dropped lower to my forearms as he closed the distance. He stood behind me, his hand caressing my bottom. "You need to feel my palm?" he asked as he lifted his hand, brought it down. The crack of it filled the room and I startled.

It wasn't all that hard of a spanking, only a slight sting accompanied it.

I closed my eyes, reveled in the feel. He gave me another playful swat, then slid his fingers over my pussy.

I cried out, tossed my head back and stared at the far wall. "Gage!" I gasped as he circled my entrance. I pushed my hips back, hoping they'd sink into me again. My pussy actually hurt. So swollen. So empty.

I knew what it was like to be filled, but only in my ass. My pussy ached being so empty, needing his cock deep to clench and squeeze, to milk every drop of his seed.

"Greedy, too," he said. While the sound was rough with need, it was playful.

"More."

He gave me another soft swat, this time to the other side of my bottom. "I'm in charge now, mate. You rule my cock, but I say when it's going to sink into that pussy."

"As long as it's now," I replied seriously. His fingers had gone beyond teasing, especially when they flicked over my clit with expert precision.

I was lifted and turned, tossed onto the bed on my back. I bounced once, then settled with my head on the pillows. Gage put one knee on the bed and moved over me, a hand on the side of my head propping him up. He grabbed his cock at the base, stroked up and down the long length.

"Like I said, mate, you rule me. Heart and soul. This cock, it's all yours. This seed?" He swiped his thumb over the tip, collected the fluid and brought it to my lips. I flicked my tongue out, licked the tangy drop. His eyes followed my action and he stopped talking, stopped breathing for a moment. "It's all for you. It's going in that pussy. I'm going to fill you with my cock, then fill you with my seed. If the gods see fit, we will make a baby this very first time."

The idea of making a baby with him had me squirming, but I was pinned in place by his dark gaze.

"But know this. You are mine. I claim you, Danielle from Earth, as my Marked Mate."

He reached down, placed my hand over his on his cock and guided it toward my entrance. I spread my legs wider so I made room for him between.

"And you are mine," I whispered.

I felt the broad head slide over my folds, felt it catch at my entrance, settle there. Our eyes met as I took his hand from his cock, held it, entwined our fingers, pressed our Marks together so the heat of it coursed through both of us.

He pressed forward, sinking into me. I couldn't look away. Wouldn't. This was the moment I became his. His cock was going where no other had been, where no other would ever go.

My eyes widened as he stretched me, watched as his darkened impossibly further. He sank in more, then more still. I caught my breath as he went all the way into me, his hips pressing into mine.

I was so full, I didn't know where Gage ended and I began. We were one.

"Mine," he growled.

I could do nothing but nod, my inner walls rippling and clenching, adjusting to his invasion. He was big and thick and hot and I had taken every inch of him.

Sweat beaded at his brow as he held himself still, as our marks pulsed in coordination with our heartbeats.

He pulled back and I gasped. He groaned. The friction made my body heat, the need to come so great. There had been no pain and I would not worry about why I didn't have any or question it now. I only saw Gage, only thought of him. Felt him. Breathed him.

"You're so tight. So hot. Wet," he murmured, shifting his hips, slowly fucking me. This wasn't playful any longer. This was...making love. The connection was real, intense. The feelings indescribable.

His strokes became longer and I began to meet him, finding our rhythm, a tempo as old as time.

"Gage, I'm going to come," I gasped when he circled over my clit, rubbing it just right.

"Come for me. Come all over my cock and I'll follow you."

I arched my back, took him deeper and did just that. I came, hard. Powerfully. I felt a bright sear of pain in my palm as I heard Gage groan, felt him thicken, then spurt deep inside.

The pleasure continued, but the mark went silent, as if the connection was complete, that we didn't need it any longer as a guide to find each other. This was where Marked Mates were supposed to be. Together. One. Seed filling my womb and continuing his line. Our destiny.

11

"Is it official?"

Katie opened the door to my dressing room and walked in wearing a gorgeous blue ball gown that brought out the color of her eyes to perfection. The A-line skirt was the hue of a dark, turbulent ocean. But the fitted top was off the shoulder and covered with a delicate and artful black appliqué lace. Lexi walked in right behind her wearing a stunning black-on-black ball gown. Her dark hair and eyes made her look like a Greek goddess.

I felt my cheeks heating at Katie's question and I turned back to stare at the stranger I saw in the mirror. Me. In a gown and not a pair of jeans and hiking boots. The dress was a champagne colored confection, silk under a tulle so fine that it looked like air. The bodice hugged my small frame. My shoulders and arms were bare, covered only in more of the sheer fabric embroidered with the most beautiful flowers I had ever seen. They flowed randomly around the gown, across the top of my breasts down to my waist and graced the hem. I loved it.

"Well?" Katie prompted.

"Yes. He's mine."

It was just before the ascension ceremony and Gage had allowed me—as if—to go off with Katie and Lexi to get dressed in our fancy gowns. Of course, Von was nearby as well as a few other guards for protection. I was thankful that my two BFFs had found a dress for me while I'd been in the med center and...well, busy with Gage.

My friends broke into squeals and rushed me, all three of our large skirts competing for space.

"Okay, okay!" I laughed at their excitement, but also because my face heated thinking about all the things Gage had done to me, all the places he'd touched and kissed and...explored. Not just the first time, but...all night long.

And how much I'd loved it. Begged him not to stop.

How could I face my friends after doing so many wicked and naughty things?

But judging by the knowing looks on both of their faces, they knew *exactly* what kind of night I'd just had.

"Bunch of lucky bitches, eh?" Katie asked, grinning.

Lexi fussed with the full skirt of my dress. "Definitely." She stepped back, shaking her head. "That dress is too good to be real."

"I know, right? Thank you guys so much for finding it for me." I spun in a circle, admiring the full skirt, the lovely champagne color that made my hair look even more golden than usual. My eyes stood out like huge pools of blue and even I had to admit, I looked like a fairy princess.

And ridiculously enough, *I was one.* "I can't believe that's me."

"Believe it." Katie smiled and raised one brow. "But we didn't pick it out. In fact, this is the first time we've seen it."

"Then who?" I asked.

"It was Mauve. I heard her talking to Gage about your gown, and Rayla's." Lexi smiled, looked as happy as I felt. "Wherever you got it, you're going to bring your man to his knees in that dress."

I giggled. I couldn't help it, and let the truth pop out. "That's where he was last night." Licking me. Tasting me. Making me beg, and squirm, and break into a million pieces so he could put me back together again.

"So was Von," Lexi said with a deadpan face. "I came twice before he would let me sit down."

The silence was deafening until I glanced at Katie and we both burst out laughing.

We were all smiling when I turned back to the mirror, still speechless at the vision staring back at me. "That is *not* me. That can't be me."

My golden hair was piled on top of my head in an elaborate up-do that had taken over an hour. I glanced over and caught Lexi watching me.

"You really do look like a princess."

Katie clapped her hands and nodded. "Ab-so-fucking-lutely."

I held out my arms and my friends stepped closer so I could pull them to my sides with my hands around their waists. We stood shoulder to shoulder and I could see all three of us in the mirror. "Look at us. We should be at Disney World. God, I remember freaking out at the Interstellar Bride processing center. If I'd known life was going to turn out to be this awesome, I would have signed up sooner."

Lexi leaned her head down on my shoulder. "Best friends for life, right? No matter what?"

"No matter what."

"No matter what," Katie said.

A second later a sharp knock on the door interrupted.

"Hello in there. Danielle? It's time to go."

Mauve.

Lexi grabbed one hand and Katie the other and I rolled my eyes. It seemed having a crazy mother-in-law wasn't solely an issue on Earth.

I took a deep breath. "Okay, let's do this."

Another knock and then the door to my dressing room opened. Mauve peeked her head around the corner. "Are you ready?"

"Yes." Taking every last ounce of strength I could from my friends, I squeezed their hands tightly, let go and walked toward my future. I had no idea how to be a princess. None. I was a wilderness guide more comfortable in a fishing boat than a ballroom. It wasn't as if I'd been given any kind of lessons on being royal. Gage didn't have any expectations for me other than being myself, but what about Mauve, the people of Everis?

Mauve stepped fully into the room, tilted her head and smiled at me. "You look lovely, dear."

Wow. That was a surprise. I'd expected a snarky response, a haughty gaze down her slim nose, but not that. I cleared my throat.

"Thank you." Glancing down at the dress, then back up at her, I said, "I can't figure out how it's so sparkly. It's like it's been glittered with pixie dust."

Mauve looked confused but shook her head before bending down to straighten an imaginary wrinkle. "Nonsense, child. That's diamond dust from the family mines."

Diamond dust?

"Holy shit." The words exploded from Katie's mouth, but Mauve's grin was hidden from my friend as Katie practically stuttered. "Did you just say she is literally wearing ground up diamonds?"

Mauve straightened, her shoulders stiffer than I had ever seen them. She looked lovely, her brown hair not yet gray, her green eyes sparkling. She was an older version of Rayla and time had been kind to her. "Our family is famous for their diamond mines. It is tradition. Gage selected the diamonds himself."

I looked down at the dress with new eyes, imagining my mate sifting through a mine, or a selection of diamonds, choosing which ones would be destroyed just so that my gown could glitter. When had he even had a chance to do that?

I looked back up at her. "That seems like a terrible waste of diamonds."

She smiled and there was nothing tame or gentle in it. I saw the political tigress, the woman Gage claimed was feared and respected as a savvy adversary in the highest political arenas. I saw the calculation and cunning and vowed I would do my best to make this woman my friend. It was a much better choice than enemy.

But hey, at least she'd be protective of any grandchildren, right?

"Exactly the point." She looked pleased, which, I guessed, was more than good enough for the moment. "And the gown will go on display in the royal museum after the ascension."

"Another tradition?" I asked.

"Yes. Your gown and Gage's suit will be displayed in the capital for all to see."

With a shrug, I admired the dress, glad to know that it wouldn't languish in a closet after the event. Besides, there was nothing I could do about it now except enjoy and appreciate how spectacular it was. I looked over my shoulder at my friends.

Lexi looked stunned. "*Diamonds Are a Girl's Best Friend.*"

Katie laughed. "And you two stopped me from calling in for that reward. Diamond dresses." She looked to Mauve. "Does Rayla have one like that, too?"

"Of course."

Lexi just shook her head and chuckled. "Knock it off. Let's go turn our best friend into a princess."

We followed Mauve out of the room, my heart beating faster than a hummingbird's wings. But one thought kept me steady, kept my chin high and my shoulders back.

Gage was waiting for me. My mate.

I would not embarrass him. I would not fail him.

No, I was going to love him, fight for him, be whatever he needed me to be. Even a princess in a fairy godmother-created gown.

I just had to do it in front of the whole planet.

No pressure. None at all.

12

EVERYONE WAS ASSEMBLED. The circle of the Seven in the center of the Everian capital's ruling council chambers was empty. As I stood in the antechamber with my fellow council members, I realized that I would be the youngest councilor in a very long time. The youngest member here.

Our leader, a wise woman in her eighties, was known for being both powerful and pragmatic. She was also nearly three times my age.

She was not to be trifled with, and I hoped she would survive for many years as the next two in line to replace her cared more about power and less about the people.

As I stood in my knee-high black boots, tightly formed black pants, black shirt and jacket adorned with all the medals and ribbons of my family's history, the weight of the moment, of the oath I was about to take, of the pain and loss of my father, threatened to buckle my knees.

I did not want to be here.

I had never wanted to be here.

My father should have lived another twenty or thirty years. Perhaps by then I would have been ready to take his lofty place. But my father had not raised me to shirk my duty. I was his son, the last of our bloodline, the only heir to over a thousand years of history.

Unless my child had already taken root in my mate's womb. The night before, I'd certainly filled her with enough of my seed to make it possible. For my people, for her, for our future children, I could and would do anything, make any sacrifice, even stand here and await my ascension.

And so I stood proudly, waiting for the one thing in my life that was mine, truly mine. The one person who made me truly happy.

A bell rang, signaling the arrival of my mate and my mother, of the official start of the ceremony. The ushers escorted the seventy-seven judges and seventy-seven senators to their seats. When that was done, a nod was given and our leader led us down the long aisle in a procession.

I was last among them, seventh in line, and as they took their places, circling the round table, I walked up to the empty seat that had belonged to my father and silence fell in the room.

With a quick glance to the side of the room, I saw my mate standing with the others.

Holy fuck, she was lovely. Regal. The perfect vision of a princess. But I knew the real Dani, the one without the diamond dust, the makeup and the styled hair. I knew her naked and open. Bare of everything but just...her. Hair wild and tangled from my fingers. Lips red not from coloring, but from my kisses. Her small hands, I knew how they felt gripping my cock. Her legs, long and lean, powerful and strong as she walked from the Touchstone to find and save me. But that was her body. It was her brain, her smarts, her keen Hunter sense, that I loved. I craved. Not that any body would do, but I would take Dani *in* any body, as along as she was mine. Beside me. With me. Beneath me.

My mother and sister were on Dani's right. Her friends, Katie and Lexi, on her left and surrounding them, Von, Bryn, Elon and a handful of other guards I recognized. Elon stood with Geoffrey and Thomar. Elon's gaze was solely on Rayla, not the proceedings before him. Luckily, the other two looked more than serious enough to make up for it, their gazes scanning the crowd for every threat. I knew Von had additional men stationed around the assembly, his Elite Hunters blending in with the rest, watching everyone and everything, determined to keep me safe.

I had pulled each and every man aside and told them to protect my mate first. Not one had argued, which had saved me from replacing any of Von's men with some of my mother's.

All eyes were on the empty table at the center of the room, the procession and ascension that only took place when one of the royal members' seats was taken by an heir. The last time all those gathered today had been in one room had been when my father stood where I stand now, ready to claim his place in history.

Me? I only had eyes for Danielle as she and the others took their seats. The sight of her took my breath away and my cock hardened in anticipation of taking that beautiful gown from her body and kissing every inch of her soft skin.

The taste of her was still on my tongue from waking her this morning, settled between her thighs, my mouth on her pussy.

I don't know how long I stared, but the leader of the Seven cleared her throat to regain my attention. As she drew a ceremonial dagger from its place at her side and laid it on the table pointed toward the center, the soft whispers that had begun to circulate the room died immediately.

"We are here today to welcome Prince Gage of Everis to his seat on the Seven." Her voice was thready with age, but clear and loud.

As she spoke, the other five around the circle drew the daggers from their sheaths at their waists and placed them on the round table in a similar fashion, blades pointing toward the middle. When they were done, she looked at me.

"Gage, son of Gandar, son of our forefather, Prince Greggor, do you accept your seat on this council and vow to uphold the laws of Everis to protect her people? Do you pledge your life, your blood, and your honor to serving Everis and this council?"

With those words, the weight of the moment bore down on me. I remembered standing here as a boy, watching my father being asked the exact same questions, take this exact same oath. It was one of my earliest memories, and also one of the most vivid because he had looked like a giant among men, like a god, so strong, so powerful. Even as a child, I'd known what was happening at the time was important. Bigger than just family. Once the oath was said, everyone on the planet had counted on him to take care of them, to do what was best, to be a true and strong leader.

That feeling of pride and awe I had felt as a boy surged to life inside me and, as I looked around those gathered in the room, I recognized what I saw reflected in their eyes. I drew my dagger from my hip, held it high as I sought and held my mate's gaze, the love I saw shining there making me stronger than I'd ever imagined possible.

There was nothing that I could not do with her by my side.

"I do. I pledge my life, my blood, my honor to serving Everis and this council."

I made my solemn vow and meant every word. My life. My blood. My honor. But not just to the people of Everis: to her.

I placed my dagger on the table and took my seat as one of the council attendants held out the gold inlaid band that would attach to my shirt collars. The elder walked around the table to place it around my neck. Murmurs from the audience began, knowing that with the vows said, this was all protocol.

I knew on other worlds their leaders wore ornate jewels and crowns on their heads, or held massive swords the size of a man. Diamond encrusted scepters. Pomp. Baubles.

But we were Hunters. I would be recognized by scent before I entered a room. I did not need a crown. In truth, I didn't need this ceremony, but the planet needed to hear my oath. The only thing I needed was Dani, by my side, in my bed, looking at me with trust in her eyes and tenderness in her touch. If she loved me, nothing else mattered.

The ceremony was being broadcast to every corner of the planet, and beyond, to the colony on Everis 8, to the green farm moon of Seladon and to every prisoner, guard, bounty hunter and judge serving on the prison moon of Incar. The broadcasts would be sent across the galaxy, to all of the Coalition planets, all the way back to Earth.

No, I did not need a crown to hold power. I stood tall, rising from my seat once the band of gold was placed around my neck. Raising my hand to address both those gathered and those watching all around the Coalition of Planets, I spoke clearly, so that no one would mistake the most important and humbling announcement of my life.

"Thank you all. As my first official act as a member of the Seven, I would like to introduce my friends, my family, my fellow Everians and all members of the Coalition to my Marked Mate, Danielle Gunderson, from the planet Earth. She has accepted my claim and the mating ceremony is complete. She is your princess."

I held out my hand to her. She looked shocked. Her cheeks turned the delightful pink usually reserved for our bed chamber and decidedly less clothing. But she was glowing, beautiful, a glittering vision as she stood and walked toward me.

Everyone in the chamber erupted in applause even as they bowed in deference. As she acknowledged them with a regal nod, her elegance flowed naturally, and I realized she was born for this, born for me.

When she stood by my side, I took her hand, lifted it to my mouth and kissed her knuckles. Once the cheers died down, I pulled her close, her arm linked with mine, before I raised my hand to silence everyone. "As my second official announcement, I would like to introduce my beautiful sister, Rayla, and her mate, the Elite Hunter Elon of Everis."

The applause was just as loud as before, for my sister was well-loved by the people. At first, she blushed at the center of attention shifting to her, but Elon strode forward swiftly, clearly eager to make her his in front of everyone, and looked to her. After giving him a brilliant smile, she took his hand and he pulled her to him. The only person with a shocked expression was my mother, whose smile was brittle. Her skin looked pale and when her gaze met mine, her eyes narrowed. I knew she would be angry at this plot that I had hatched with my sister. But Rayla had felt strongly that the public announcement was the only way to thwart our mother's attempts to assure a politically advantageous match for her. Rayla's fate was now sealed, and I hoped it was with a lifetime of happiness.

Elon escorted Rayla to stand behind me, her smile radiant. He leaned down, kissed her and swung her in the air, her blue colored gown twirling like a glittering cloud. The applause echoed off the walls of the chamber.

Beside me, Dani squeezed my arm. I turned to her. She stood on tiptoe and whispered, "Diamonds? Seriously?"

I grinned as I let my gaze roam over her gown, admiring the way it curved to accentuate her small breasts and narrow waist, the soft womanly flare of her hips.

Kissing here, in the council chamber, was a breach of protocol, at least for a member of the Seven. A brush of my lips on her knuckles was one thing, but the kiss I gave her, on the lips and with a fair amount of tongue, was something else entirely. But I would be my own prince and I would make my own protocols. Showing appropriate affection for my mate would show the depth of our love, the bond with family, that was important for the entire planet to witness.

"There is not a diamond that exists more beautiful than you are," I murmured.

Then I joined Elon, who had yet to allow my sister to come up for air.

Although, the woman wasn't complaining. She was, in fact, clinging to him like he was her heart and soul, her everything. I could not envy him, but I was eager to join him.

Framing Dani's delicate face in my hands, I kissed her again. Claimed her. There was nothing shy in the kiss, I held nothing back.

My mate, my fierce, fearless mate, kissed me back like she'd never get enough, like I was her life and she didn't care who was watching.

I'd never loved her more than I did in that moment.

As the assembly cheered, I knew I would be seen as a young, foolish man compared to the staunch, elder members of the Council of the Seven. But I didn't care. She was my Marked Mate. A miracle who would give others hope.

And I would not deny myself this pleasure.

13

THE BALCONY where I stood overlooked the most lavish ballroom I'd ever seen. Mauve had outdone herself and *everything* glittered. The flowers. Our gowns. Even the elaborate and elegant chandeliers hanging over our guests. They sparkled as if lit from within by a thousand stars, and I imagined that they, too, were diamonds, not crystal or glass. Insane!

God, Gage was rich. He'd told me as much, told me he was a prince, heir to the seat on the Seven, a royal bloodline that they could trace back for over a thousand years.

And I'd believed him. I had.

But seeing was *believing*. The family wealth, the respect, the pomp and circumstance surrounding his ascension to his seat? I was a middle-class girl from a small town. Not an alien princess. Wearing a fancy dress was one thing, but this? I felt like a fish out of water, the ugly duckling surrounded by swans. Every cliché I could think of was rattling around inside my head. And worse, when I looked in the mirror, I didn't recognize myself. This beautiful dress wasn't mine. The fancy hair wasn't me. I was a jeans and t-shirt kind of girl. Casual ponytail and sneakers. I did *not* take an hour to do my hair, let alone have someone do it for me.

And I did *not* wear dresses covered in diamond dust. Dust, yes. Diamonds? Hell, no.

Standing alone, looking over a ballroom full of wealthy Everians, of judges and senators and other royals I'd met in passing but couldn't remember their names, my stomach was in my throat. One night, I'd thought. One night and I could go back to just being *me.*

The longer I stared at the smiling women, the Hunters prowling around the edges of the room, their gazes roaming over each one of them, even the scent of power and money and privilege in the room, I realized it was never going to end. This was my new life. Was this *really* Gage's?

"I don't belong here." I was thinking out loud, but the large, warm hands that wrapped around me from behind alerted me that my new mate, my *prince,* had heard every word. I sensed him, knew him. *Scented* him and I was relieved. Soothed by his presence, his touch. His comforting —and firm—hold.

"You are the only one who does belong here," he murmured in my ear, his breath fanning my neck. "This is your home now. Our home."

"I'm not used to living in a home that has a *ballroom.* Can't we just go back to our bedroom?" I angled my head to the side to give his lips better access. "That room I like very much, especially with you in it."

He growled as he kissed my neck. "Ballroom now, bedroom later."

I sighed at the promise in those words. "All right. But I don't fit in with these people. I don't know anything about politics or what they all expect. I haven't been on this planet for very long. I don't know how to be a princess." There, I'd said it, admitted my biggest fear...that I'd fail him.

"I don't want them, Dani." He leaned down, his chin resting on my shoulder as we watched the sway and current of the party, the dancing, the flirting and deal-making. "You are real. You care about me, not my money or position or family history. You are mine and I am yours." His arms tightened around me, his embrace solid, sure. "You are the only one in this room I care about."

I leaned into his warmth, let his touch soothe me as I laughed. "That's because Elon stole Rayla away to have his wicked way with her." I'd laughed at the shocked expression on my new sister's face when her mate had said their good-byes, thrown her over his shoulder and carted her out of the ascension ceremony. Even I knew it wasn't proper etiquette, but still. It was somewhat romantic: Elon publicly and blatantly claiming her for his own. I guessed he didn't want anyone to doubt that it was...*official.* And the longer they were away from the party, the *more* official it became.

With a playful growl in my ear, Gage pressed his hard cock into my back so there would be no mistaking his own interest. "As I should be doing with you, mate. I should toss you over my shoulder and have my way with you, fuck you in a dark corner somewhere."

A thrill shot through me at the very idea. "Please?" I asked.

He laughed softly. "I have turned you into an insatiable wench."

I turned my head to the side, so he could kiss me. He took the hint, so in tune with me that I still couldn't grasp the fact that he was real. Here. Mine. His arms around me. Loving me. For so long he'd been nothing more than a dream. Not the dream sharing, but the dream of having a man of my own, who loved me, cherished me, put me first. I'd had that for years on Earth, never imagined it happening.

"You have. So, the dark corner? Hmmm. Where would you start, I wonder?" I blinked slowly, opening my eyes to stare up at the man I'd come to love more than my own heart beating.

"Start?" Lowering his forehead to mine, he held my gaze. "I'd start by sliding this dress off your body one delicate curve at a time, kissing every single part of you as it is revealed."

I licked my lips and let him see the fire he was kindling starting in my gaze. "And then?"

"I'd drop to my knees, spread open those soft, wet, pink pussy lips and devour your sweet juices until your fingers are buried in my hair and you're whimpering my name. Coming all over my tongue."

My grin felt devilish, and I knew we were catching the attention of the crowd below, but I didn't care. The idea of his head between my legs again had me rubbing my thighs together to ease the ache. It wasn't working. "Whimpering? Not screaming?"

He chuckled, pulling me close, so close his heat scorched even through all of our clothes. "The screaming comes later, mate, when your legs are wrapped around my hips and your pussy is squeezing my hard cock, milking all my seed from my balls."

I closed my eyes with a soft moan and lifted on tiptoe to close the small space between us, my lips brushing his as I whispered, "I'll hold you to that, my prince. And soon."

My kiss was soft and tender, not meant to stoke his passion, but to let him know that I was his, that no one else in this room mattered more to me. That he was right. I didn't care about diamonds or dresses or who his father had been. Gage was mine. That was the only thing that mattered to me.

Lips still touching, Gage whispered back. "Like I said, ballroom then bedroom. Shall we enter the fray?"

I sighed. "I can hardly wait." I left him to wonder if I meant about joining the party or getting back to our room and getting him between my thighs.

"Let's dance." He twirled me out of his arms as if we'd been dancing a waltz, then pulled me back in.

I laughed at the playfulness and I was out of breath. I could track a mountain lion or a bear, but dancing?

"Dancing isn't one of my specialties." And with this dress? These shoes? They weren't four-inch, spike heels, but they weren't hiking boots either.

"Nonsense, mate. All you have to do is hold on. I shall lead, shall take care of you as I always will."

Smiling so hard my face was beginning to hurt, I realized I'd never been this happy. I held his hand as he led me down the curving, grand staircase to the ballroom floor where a slow, dreamy song was being played on stringed instruments that looked oddly similar to those on Earth. He pulled me close, lifted me off my feet, and swirled me around the room as if I were floating on a cloud. I kissed the side of his neck. "You're right. This dancing stuff is easy."

Everything was fine, until I lost a shoe. It flew into the groin of one of the judges, an ancient Everian who was ninety if he was a day. "I'm so sorry!"

He grunted, then smiled as his much younger companion, a young man who looked like he must be a grandson, bent down to pick up the shoe and held it out to me. Gage took it from his hand before I could react. "Thank you, Zandor."

"My pleasure." The young man looked at me with something I recognized as desire in his eyes as Gage knelt at my feet, slipping the wayward shoe back into place.

The old man's face was lined with wrinkles, his dark gray eyes filled with humor as he stared down at my mate. "Don't do that, Son. Don't reload the cannon. She has quite the aim."

Gage froze under my hand, his shoulder stiff until he slid the shoe in place, lowered my foot to the floor and burst into laughter. "I'll try to be more careful where I set my target, my lord."

The elder was stooped, but his shoulders were broad, his bearing regal and I reassessed his age to be at least a century. Maybe more, which was insane because I didn't think I'd ever seen one so elderly out and about. Only on TV for being the oldest person on Earth.

Gage stood and bowed at the waist. "Prince Zaylen, young prince Zandor, may I introduce my beautiful mate,

Danielle. Danielle, this is Prince Zaylen, who resigned from the Seven last year. He is well missed at the circle table. And this is his grandson, heir to a seat on the council of the Seven."

The young man reached eagerly for my hand, but his grandfather swatted him away like a fly and took his place, his touch gentle, his kiss to the back of my hand very formal, yet friendly. I laughed when I saw the flustered look on his grandson's face, his pink cheeks, and the satisfied look on Gage's. Prince Zaylen chuckled and murmured, "Age before beauty, Zandor."

"Of course, sir." The young prince was probably around twenty years old, young and obviously in his prime. He was handsome, with fair looks—blond hair and green eyes—which I was sure attracted many young ladies to his side. But not me. He looked like a child next to my mate, a child who had yet to master his impulses. Learn the level of respect necessary for his lofty future position.

Gage made small talk with the elderly prince for a few minutes before we were pulled away to a new introduction, a new family, a new name.

"That's a lot of Z's," I commented as we strolled.

"Tradition. As you heard at the ascension ceremony, I am from a family of G's."

I thought about it as we continued along. "So that means I have to think of a G name for our first child?"

Gage stopped and turned to face me. Tilted my chin up. "Mate, do you know something I don't?" he asked, eyes serious, the swirl of the ball around us forgotten.

"What? No. It's too soon. I just want to make sure I don't fall in love with the name Joshua or Olivia."

He smiled then, leaned in and kissed my forehead. It was so tender I ached with the love from it. "I am pleased to hear you thinking this way, that perhaps we have already made this child you are wanting to name."

I huffed out a little laugh.

"The answer is yes. Our children should have names that begin with G to honor those who came before."

Grace. Garrison. Gus. Gabrielle. Those were all good. "I can live with a G-named child, as long as I make him...or her, with you."

He gave me a brilliant smile before guiding me back through the throng. Names. Faces. More names. More faces. I was getting a serious headache until Rayla swooped over to us, looking flushed and absolutely glowing with happiness. God, I knew that feeling, knew it well. It was probably because she and Elon had completed one—or more—steps toward claiming Rayla's three virginities. I glanced up at Gage, whose scowl told me he assumed the same thing. I loved that he was such a protective older brother, but he would have to learn to let go. And pronto.

"Don't worry," Rayla began. "Mother's got a book, a real paper book that you can carry around with everyone's name, face and entire life history to keep track of who's who. I'll be shocked if you don't find it on your bedside table when you retire for the night."

"Seriously?" I asked.

"Never underestimate Mother when it comes to machinations or scheming, dear sister. She's a goddess." Rayla smiled as I pulled her into a hug, pressing my lips close to her ear so no other would hear, even Gage. No, especially Gage.

"Are you well? *Things* went well with Elon?"

"The best." When I pulled back to look in her eyes, I saw what I needed to see. Pink cheeks from a tinge of embarrassment, but the look of a well-satisfied woman. "If I'd known it was going to be that good, I would have thrown him down and had my way with him months ago."

"Behave, mate." Elon came up to her side looking well-pleased and content. Yes, at least one of her virginities was gone. I wondered if that's how others viewed Gage and me, although Gage had stated outright at the ascension ceremony that the full claiming was complete. Did we look this happy? Did I radiate joy as Rayla did? Did I have the same glow of a well-satisfied woman?

Closing my eyes, I took stock, letting everything going on inside me register. I felt the slight tenderness between my thighs from my first time. Gage had been gentle, but he'd taken me more than once. I'd wanted it, needed it as much as he. I wasn't sore, but deliciously well-used and I wouldn't wish a ReGen wand to make it go away. The feeling was a reminder that I was Gage's. No one else's.

Yes. Yes, there was no doubt I looked just as satisfied and loved as Rayla. And her gown was stunning, a mark of Gage's family, and I had to agree that we both looked like princesses straight out of a fairy tale with strong, handsome mates by our sides.

"You!" Rayla said, stepping up to Gage and pushing her finger into his chest. "I want to give you a piece of my mind. You were supposed to tell Mother first and *then* announce our mating."

"Where would be the fun in that?" Gage chuckled.

It made me smile even before his warm hand settled around my back to rest on the curve of my hip. His touch warmed me to my core, his scent enveloping me like a drug and just that quickly I was wet and eager for him, knew I always would be.

"And you," she leaned into her mate, her mock anger a complete farce and we all knew it. "You were *not* supposed to throw me over your shoulder and drag me off like one of Dani's *cave dwellers* at an ascension ceremony of all places!"

"Cave dwellers?" Elon turned his attention to me, but I was laughing too hard to answer, so Gage did it for me.

"I think you mean a *caveman,* little sister."

Elon's shock had not faded. "Men live in caves on Earth? I knew they were primitive, but caves?"

I nodded as Gage winked, then took him by the shoulder, leading him toward a beverage station on the side of the room. I linked arms with my new sister and we followed them as I listened to Gage explain to his fellow *caveman*, exactly what we Earth women meant by the term.

A feast awaited. Everything I could possibly imagine, from sweets to fruits and candy confections I had never tried, but tasted suspiciously similar to dark chocolate, were laid out along one entire wall of the ballroom with servants and Hunters both stationed every few steps: one to serve the food, the other to guard Gage. And me, I supposed. "The food looks amazing. Your mother really outdid herself."

"Our mother," Rayla insisted. She looked at the feast with a sigh. "I wish my stomach were larger. There are so many choices, and Elon wore me out. I'm starving."

I laughed, my own stomach rumbling. "Me, too."

"Speaking of Mother, where is she?" Rayla stood on tiptoe, craning her neck to see over the heads of men neither one of us had a chance in hell of looking over. "This is her crowning moment. She would never miss it."

I had turned to look for her when a familiar voice interrupted us from behind.

"Ladies, if we may?" I turned to see Geoffrey and Thomar had come up behind us dressed resplendently in Gage's family colors, black and champagne gold.

Rayla tilted her head, her glance darting to inspect Elon's humorous expression as the meaning of being a caveman dawned.

"He'll probably be proud of it, like your brother," I offered.

"Without doubt." She grinned and we shared a smile, a sister smile, one full of secrets and hidden truths. I'd never had a sister, but now, with Rayla, I had one more thing to be grateful for. Turning to Geoffrey, she was still smiling. "How may we help you, Hunters?"

I had learned the address of 'Hunter' was equivalent to calling someone a true gentleman back home. It was a compliment and a title all in one.

Both men bowed low, but Geoffrey spoke. "May we have the honor of a dance?"

Rayla glanced at Elon, who gave her an imperceptible nod, then held out her hand immediately to Thomar. "Of course." As he led her toward the dance floor, she grinned at me. "I could use a little more of the cave dweller mentality later tonight."

With a laugh at what I knew seeing us in another Hunter's arms would do to our mates, I looked to Gage. While he knew I was his—no one else's—I wanted to make sure he didn't go all caveman if I danced with another male. He smiled and nodded as well, so I took Geoffrey's outstretched hand. We followed the other two into the throng of dancing couples. I glanced over my shoulder, saw

Gage watching me. Specifically, he was watching my ass with that dark, intent gaze. I wouldn't mind a little caveman action tonight either and I was going to ensure it happened. I wasn't a virgin any longer and I could certainly seduce my own mate. It seemed pretty easy; all I had to do was get naked and he'd pounce.

age

CONTENTMENT. That was this feeling. Happiness.

Peace.

I had no idea what I'd been missing until she showed up magically...miraculously in my sleep. On Everis. Then there was no going back.

Dani was mine, the claiming complete. I had taken my rightful place on the council of Seven and I knew my father would be proud. Life. Blood. Honor. I had pledged them all to my people and the beautiful woman swirling on Geoffrey's arm.

Many, many Hunters' eyes followed my mate as she circled the room, a vision of gold and diamonds. I had never imagined a woman could look so beautiful. I wanted to tear her from Geoffrey's arms and carry her off to some dark corner, lift the long hem of her dress and sink into her. I wanted to wrinkle the fabric, muss her hair, smear her lipstick so everyone knew she'd been ravished, that she was taken.

Perhaps Elon felt the same way, for he stood stiffly beside me, watching Rayla dance with Thomar. I hated the idea he put his hands on my sister, but he was in love. That was the only thing keeping me from punching him in the face.

I grinned, knowing we were love-struck, greedy mates.

I turned to one of the servers and asked for two shots of their strongest drink. We were both going to need it to survive the night. For I knew that although Geoffrey was the first to dance with his new princess, *my princess,* he would not be the last. I caught young prince Zandor watching Rayla and Thomar swirl about the dance floor, waiting for his own chance, but nearly laughed when the elder Zaylen beat him to it, the old man tapping young Thomar on the shoulder and taking Rayla into his arms. He danced well for one of his age. I hoped to be like him when the time came, swirling Dani about, our children and grandchildren around us.

"Gods help me," Elon groaned next to me and turned his head away, fists clenched. "I can't watch. I want to punch a ninety-year-old man."

I did laugh then, for my mark had calmed with the claiming complete. Finally. But I knew the fire that burned in Elon's body, his soul. Until Rayla was wholly and completely his, controlling his instinct to conquer her would be difficult, even if she were in the arms of a man almost five times her age.

Geoffrey and Dani swirled just out of sight behind several taller Hunters and their dance partners, and I took the two sturdy drinks from the attendant's tray and handed one of them to Elon. I raised my glass. "To our mates. The two most beautiful women in the room."

Elon slammed his entire drink back and asked the attendant for another.

I grinned, held up my fingers. "Make it two."

The servant hurried away as Thomar walked back to us, a slightly shamed look on his face. "Put aside for an nonagenarian."

Elon laughed this time, yelling after the attendant to bring not two, but three shots of alcohol before turning back to me. "I suppose we should have mated unappealing harpies instead. Gone off to live in one of your Dani's Earth caves so we wouldn't have to share."

My smile was tolerant and I had no wish to argue, or state the obvious. Neither one of us would trade our mate for another. Both females might have sharp tongues and be ridiculously stubborn, but I was proud of Dani. Fiercely protective. Loyal to my dying breath. She'd walked into the room and charmed every member of the Seven, been kind to everyone since our arrival at the palace. I dared believe even my mother was warming to her, which was a remarkable feat. In just two days, she'd managed to charm everyone in the palace. "It wouldn't have mattered, Elon. Already the staff prefer her to me."

Thomar chuckled. "At the risk of you stabbing me with your ceremonial dagger, may I say you're not nearly as pretty as she is, my prince."

"That is the absolute truth."

The attendant returned with our drinks and I finished

mine in one gulp as Rayla appeared from the throng and immediately pressed herself to Elon's side. He settled at once, his arm going around her, the edgy impatience of his stance calming. His world was right once more.

I knew the feeling and wanted it for myself. Where was Dani? She'd been appeasing the other guests for more than long enough. It was my fucking turn.

Rayla took the glass from her mate's hand and swallowed the contents as Thomar, perhaps a little in love with my sister, watched, in awe.

"Where is Mother?" Rayla asked me. "I haven't seen her all evening, and you know she would never miss her own party."

Her words struck home like a dagger, my instincts flaring to life in an almost violent surge. I'd been so preoccupied with my mate, the obsession of my cock buried deep in her tight, wet heat, that I hadn't been paying attention to the rest of the world. Only Dani.

Elon picked up on my unease at once, his lips thinning as he quickly scanned the room. Thomar put his drink in Rayla's hand, untouched. "I will collect Geoffrey and we will find her at once."

"Thank you, Thomar." I wanted to look for my mother, but there was one female even more important to me. I looked at Rayla as Thomar disappeared into the crowd. "Where is Dani?"

She shrugged, sipping the second glass a bit more slowly. "Last I saw, she was dancing with Geoffrey near the balcony."

The balcony was on the opposite side of the ballroom with open doors to the exterior. With the throng of people, it would take me several minutes to get there.

"Damn it," I growled. "I should have told Geoffrey to keep her on this side of the room."

"You would have him only dance in half the room? He'd be tripping over everyone. There is a system, brother. A natural flow."

"I don't care," I growled.

I had a strange feeling growing within me, a foreboding, but I fought it down. I was being overly protective. Paranoid. We were surrounded by Hunters. Von's men. Mine. She was fine. Just because I couldn't see her, didn't mean she wasn't safe. And yet... "I shouldn't have let her leave my side. Not for a moment."

Elon leaned down and kissed Rayla gently on the lips. "Who's the cave dweller now, mate?"

She smiled at him, her eyes glowing with happiness. "Oh, I knew my big brother was a beast all along." Taking his chin between her fingertips, she pushed up on tiptoes and kissed him, not quite as gently. "You, however, are *my* cave dweller."

"Damn right, I am."

"Do not leave her side, Elon. That is an order."

His head snapped up as he caught my tension. I wasn't the only man here whose instincts were being blocked by a warm, willing female.

I didn't wait for him to comment before diving into the throng of people, taking a direct route to my mate, ignoring well-wishers and political climbers by the dozens. I didn't have time to talk. My Hunter senses flared. My mate senses flared. Something was wrong. The knowledge was burning inside me, growing stronger with each step I took toward my mate.

Dani

Dancing with Geoffrey was awkward, and I couldn't fully relax in his hold. He wasn't Gage, and he was stiff, nervous. His hand on my waist felt wrong somehow, like it didn't belong. It was strange, as I'd never felt like a prude before, even when I was a virgin, but now that I wasn't, I would have thought interacting with men would be easier. Not harder.

Boy, was I wrong. Now that I knew Gage's touch, the pleasure of his kiss, his hard body, his cock, I didn't want to touch anyone else. *Be touched* by anyone else. Maybe it was a Marked Mate thing. Maybe it was Geoffrey. Maybe it was just me. I had no idea. All I knew was that his hand holding mine was clammy and sweaty, his body was stiff, and he was making me nervous.

I felt bad for him, that he was so awkward, but perhaps he just needed to dance more. To interact with some Everian women. Hopefully, he'd find his Marked Mate and it would be easy for him. To let their marks handle the hard part and they'd just know they were perfect for each other.

I was becoming weary from all the excitement of the day. Loud music, lots of people. I wasn't used to such pomp and fanfare. Even worse, being the center of attention. And, wearing a dress and makeup and heels. Perhaps next time I wore a floor length gown I'd wear a sensible pair of boots beneath.

I wanted my mate, our bed, and some serious down time. I wanted Gage. Wrapped around me, holding me, making the rest of the world go away. Quiet, where I could hear his breathing, the beat of his heart.

"My apologies, Princess. I am a bit nervous." His confession should have been endearing. Instead, it made my nerves go up a notch.

"It's all right. I've never danced at a royal ball before either."

He smiled, but it didn't reach his eyes. "You look very beautiful. And you are a very kind person. Everyone at the palace is talking about their wonderful new princess."

Small talk and compliments. Neither one was something I was overly comfortable with. I knew better than to believe all of it. I was the princess so everything surely had a filter. Only positive words would be shared around me otherwise they feared for their positions. Or, maybe they feared for their lives; knowing Gage, he'd rip the head off of anyone who wanted to harm me, even verbally.

"Thank you." What else could I say? I wasn't one for small talk, especially with someone I didn't really want to *have* small talk with, so I kept it simple. Thank you was enough. I glanced over my shoulder, looked for Gage on the outer edges of the dancing. "Maybe we should head back to the others now. I'm sure Rayla will be expecting a dance now that you've spoiled me." It was rubbish, pure garbage I was spewing, but he seemed to appreciate the effort. His laugh was low, and not very loud.

"I highly doubt that. She only has eyes for Elon."

"He's a good man," I confirmed. "And he loves her."

"Both very true."

We were on the opposite side of the ballroom now, the doors open to the balcony where a cool breeze drifted in to dispel some of the heat. I took a deep breath, enjoying the colder air. The outdoors called to me as if I were in Montana, not the far reaches of the galaxy. Geoffrey noticed.

"Would you like to step onto the balcony for a moment? Cool off?"

It was tempting. So tempting. I looked over the crowd of Hunters and judges, councilors and pretty people. The men were all so tall that I couldn't see over their heads, but Gage was on the other side of that mess somewhere, and taking a moment to breathe before fighting our way back over to him seemed like an excellent idea.

I turned to Geoffrey to find him holding out his arm, elbow crooked, like a true gentleman. With a relieved smile, I put my arm through his and he led me out onto the balcony. The sun was setting, the twin moons slowly rising on the horizon in a scene straight out of a sci-fi movie. But this wasn't a movie, this was my life now. My crazy, amazing, wonderful life. It was as if I were in a sci-fi Disney movie. Surreal and yet so perfect. "It's so beautiful here."

The guards at the doors offered me a small bow, then nodded to Geoffrey as we passed. There were more Hunters on the balcony, two at the top of each set of stairs keeping guard.

Geoffrey led me to the edge where a gorgeous stone-carved railing rose to my hips as we looked out over the gardens. They were substantial; going on in a mix of mazes and formal squares, curves and decorative twists with shrubbery as far as I could see. I'd seen pictures of the Palace of Versailles, of the gardens with hedges three times the height of a man with fountains and statues and the same kind of mazes. That was nothing compared to this. The greenery stretched far into the distance, the crisp, cool air a reminder that by morning they would all be covered in frost.

It made me wonder as to the seasons, whether they had

a true summer here, if the leaves on the trees changed and fell. If they changed even to reds and oranges and yellows. Did it snow? So much to learn and I looked forward to learning it all, having Gage to show it to me.

As I was lost in thought, Geoffrey pulled what looked like a ReGen wand from his pocket and placed it in front of my body, running it briefly over my abdomen.

I glanced down at it, noticed it was similar to the ones the doctor had used after treating my ankle. It didn't hurt, whatever he was doing. "What are you doing? I'm not injured."

He ignored me, looking down at the odd device. His sigh was almost sad. "You are pregnant, Princess."

My heart skipped a beat.

"What?" How could the sensor detect that? It was impossible. Well, not exactly impossible, but we'd made love just last night. It hadn't even been twenty-four hours. "That's crazy! There's no way you can know that."

He turned the device to me and I saw the report, the scientific terminology foreign to me, but I recognized two words, *gestation* and *male*. "That device can tell me I'm pregnant and that it's a boy? How can you possibly know it's a boy?"

"DNA scans don't lie."

"And you scanned my son, who has theoretically existed for less than a day, through my body?"

He tilted his head, his look condescending, full of dislike. The nervousness was gone. "This isn't Earth, Danielle Gunderson. I had hoped to leave you out of this, as you are an innocent female, but you carry the heir."

I frowned, stepped back.

"Because it's a boy?" I was so confused. Why was Geoffrey, a guard, assessing whether I was having a baby?

"Because it's Gage's child," he replied. His tone no longer held the neutral demeanor from our time dancing. "Boy or girl, it would make no difference."

Well, now was an odd time to feel relieved that, if I had a daughter, she would inherit Gage's seat on the Seven, equal to a son, but the creepy look in Geoffrey's eyes was freaking me out. This whole thing was. I didn't actually believe him. I mean, I'd just had sex for the first time less than twelve hours before. I cleared my throat, pasted on a fake smile. "I think I'll go back inside now."

He shook his head and I spun on my heel, walked toward the doors to find them closed. I ran to the handles, pulled. Locked. We were locked out. I whirled to face Geoffrey, sick with dread, looking for the guards who had stood at the top of the stairs. Gone. They were no longer at their posts and my stomach twisted in knots, sick with the knowledge, the suspicions filling my head.

It was like there'd been a missing puzzle piece and I'd found it. Once I put it in place, the big picture made sense. *Oh god.*

"It was you, wasn't it?" I asked, my voice catching.

"What are you talking about, Princess?" From him, the title sounded like a curse, the way he hissed.

I shook my head. "Don't call me that."

"It's what you are," he countered. His hands fisted at his sides. "Gage's precious princess."

Oh fuck. He was an Elite Hunter. Fast. So damn fast I couldn't outrun him on foot or even a bicycle, let alone in a heavy ball gown and heels. "What are you going to do? Kill me?"

He shook his head. He was nervous no longer, his intent clear now, his plan in place. *Now* I could see why he'd been nervous. Getting me out here, alone, had been his intention. Now that he'd succeeded—

"Oh, no, Princess. I won't kill you yet. Not until you and the old bitch have served your purpose."

Old bitch?

Desperate, I opened my mouth to scream, but Geoffrey's Hunter speed truly was impressive, one hand covered my mouth and the other wrapped around my throat before I'd finished drawing in the air I needed to do so. His face was close to mine, so close I could see the cold, calculated fury in his eyes. He wasn't insane. He was a stone-cold killer. He'd been the one to kidnap Gage, brutalize him and leave him for dead.

Oh God.

"Shhh, Princess. You can scream all you want soon enough. Not yet, or I'll break your pretty neck and let Gage find your corpse in his bed."

I nodded that I understood, not because I had any intention of giving in to this psycho, but because it wasn't just me he could hurt, not anymore. I had a son growing inside me. Gage's child. Mine. And I loved him the moment I discovered he existed. And I believed Geoffrey's sensor now. He'd want to know the truth, to make the end result that much crueler.

"That's better," Geoffrey crooned.

There was something there, something I'd seen and ignored. Something so obvious, yet we'd all missed it. No, not all. Lexi had seen it, that very first day. *He looks a lot like you, Gage, especially when he scowls like that.*

He was scowling now, and I was shocked that no one

had seen the resemblance between Geoffrey and Gage. That *I* hadn't seen it. Lexi had said the words to Gage the first time we'd seen Geoffrey on the comms screen with Elon and Thomar. With Rayla and Mauve. Same eyes. Same dark hair. Same lips. Hatred in his eyes instead of love, but I recognized him now, knew what he was.

I licked my lips, said the words that I knew were true, even without a DNA sensor. "You're his brother, aren't you?"

He laughed, but it was cold and goosebumps rose on my arms.

"Very smart. Beautiful, too." Satisfaction. Admiration. Something dark and filled with lust passed through his eyes. "Maybe I'll rid you of the parasite in your womb and keep you for myself."

Now that my brain had kicked back on, all kinds of terrible things were spinning around in there. Bile rose in my throat.

"Did you...did you kill his father? *Your* father?"

"Of course." He kept one hand around my neck and pressed me flat to the cold stone wall of the palace. I wondered what the hell he was planning on doing, my mind racing. I knew I needed to keep him talking. Gage would notice I was missing. He would come for me. I just had to survive. Survive. Stall. Two things. I could do that, even in this deathtrap of a dress. It wasn't so pretty now, the sparkles and the long skirt, it would never look beautiful again. Not after what I just learned, now that I knew I might die in this dress. Now that I knew the kind of man Geoffrey was. A killer.

I was the nervous one now. The one with the sweaty palms. "Why? Why would you do that?"

"You'll know the truth soon enough." It was the last

thing he said to me before he lifted the strange medical gadget to my head, the same one the doctor had used to put me to sleep when I had surgery on my ankle.

And just like in the medical office, I blinked and then...nothing.

15

WHEN I WOKE, my head was being cradled in someone's lap, soft, gentle fingers strumming through my hair. It was soothing, comforting, and I didn't want to open my eyes.

But I did. Because Geoffrey was going to hurt Gage. I had to stop him.

With a jolt, I tried to sit up, my head spinning.

"Shhh. You're going to have a headache, dear. It's from the anesthesia he used to knock you out. It tastes like metal on your tongue, but it goes away in a few minutes. I'm so sorry." The female voice was one I recognized, and so were the metal bars of the cage we both sat in.

"Oh my god. Mauve? Are you all right?"

"I'm fine."

We were back in the cave: the cave where I'd found Gage. And Mauve was right, the room gradually stopped spinning, and my mouth did taste like I'd been chewing on nails. Apparently, Geoffrey hadn't repaired the chains, or bought new ones, simply thrown the helpless women into the cage and left them.

Either he thought we couldn't get out of the cage, or he didn't care.

"How far are we from the palace?"

Mauve shook her head. "I don't know, exactly. Gage's father never allowed me to come out here, and I had no desire to. It's a relic of a more brutal past, one Everians have worked centuries to forget."

Well, that was interesting. So humans weren't the only barbarians in the galaxy after all. I sighed and stood, shaking out my dress, thankful for the layers. It was cold, the sun long past setting. The twin moons that had been newly rising when I went onto the balcony with Geoffrey were now halfway through their arc in the sky. I guessed that half the night was gone.

She was crying, the tears silent but glittering like diamonds on her cheekbones. "I'm sorry. I'm so sorry."

"Why are you sorry? You didn't do this."

"In a way, I did, child. I did. I knew Gage's father loved another. I knew, but loved him. I couldn't let him go."

"What?" I didn't have time for this, for placing blame or trying to talk Gage's mother out of whatever guilt-trip she was on. "We have to get out of here." I shook the chain, stood up and pulled against it, testing the bolts that secured it to the rock walls. Stupid to wish now that Gage had shot both ends. If I could get it off the wall, I could use it as a weapon. But no. It wouldn't budge. "Where is he? Where's Geoffrey?"

"He went back to kill Gage. We're just the bait, I'm afraid."

"No." This was not happening. I would *not* be the lure that led to Gage's death.

"I'm so sorry."

"Stop saying that. We are not dying, and neither is Gage."

Mauve shook her head. Her beautiful gown, sprinkled with diamond dust, just like mine and Rayla's, was torn and dirty. Her normally regal face looked drawn and worn and she looked much older than when I'd seen her last. Old, and broken.

I leaned down in front of her and lifted her chin so she would look into my eyes. "We are getting out of here. Do you hear me? I tracked Gage to this cave. I'm the one who found him. I'm not helpless. I'm a Hunter, too. So are you. We'll figure out a way to get out of here and then we'll warn Gage. Are we clear? No one is dying." Except Geoffrey, but I wasn't going to mention that. I had no doubt that he'd be gone from this world for what he'd done. And the bastards who locked the door on me? The men at the top of the stairs? I closed my eyes and thought of each and every one of them, committing every detail possible to memory, burning them into my brain for later.

Gage was mine, a tender lover, an amazing man, but this? Kidnapping and threatening his Marked Mate and his mother? This Gage would not forgive.

I found I didn't want him to. Maybe it was the Hunter blood in me, but fury roared to life inside me, not despair. If Gage didn't get to him first, I'd find a way to kill Geoffrey myself, for threatening me, my mate, my *son,* my *family.* They were mine. Even Mauve.

"Okay, Mom. Get up. We've got to move."

"Mom?"

"Yes, you're mine now, so get used to it."

She actually laughed but reached her aged hand up so I could pull her to her feet. "I can see now why Gage is in love with you. You are a good match."

I had my new mother's approval. I'd told myself it didn't matter, but I found myself pulling her to me for a hug anyway. "I haven't had a mother in a very long time."

"I am honored to have you, Daughter. And I'm sorry if I was abrupt. I love Rayla and Gage, both. I wanted what was best for them. That's all. You were unexpected."

I squeezed her, hard, then stepped back, turning to inspect the door. "I know. I'm sorry I ruined your plans. But Rayla is totally in love with Elon, and I love your son, so you'd better roll with it."

"I will roll."

The odd response made me smile, but not as much as inspecting the lock on the door. Same stupid slide bolt. Geoffrey must have found the bolt where I'd thrown it across the room after freeing Gage. "God, he must think women are stupid."

Either that, or our escape was irrelevant to his plans. The second possibility more likely than the first.

I pulled the bolt free and unlocked the door. Swinging it wide, I stepped out of the cage, Mauve right behind me. We walked together, arm in arm, to the cave entrance to take stock of our situation. It was cold. Dark. Miles of rugged mountain terrain stretched out before us. And we were in gowns and heels. Not ideal.

But I'd been here before. I'd tracked Gage through these mountains. I mentally retraced my steps, thought about where we might hide until my mate came for us. Because he would come. I knew he would come. We just had to survive until then.

"We can't stay here." If Geoffrey came back, I wasn't going to be a sitting duck, waiting for him to kill us.

"But where can we go?"

I slipped off one high-heeled shoe, then the other. Bending down, I reached up beneath my dress and tore some of the underlying, diamond-free silk from the lining, enough to wrap one foot. "Take off your shoes. We're going to wrap our feet in silk. It'll make it harder for him to track our footsteps."

Mauve did the best she could, but she was older, and spent her life in the capital, not the mountains. But she did as I said and I helped her tie make-shift silk sandals around her feet. It wasn't the best, but it was better than nothing.

"Let's go. Stay close, and don't talk above a whisper, no matter what you hear."

"Lead the way, Dani. I'm with you. I'll try to keep up."

I nodded and started down the hill to the trail I'd followed to get here. I knew it was away from the palace, toward the Touchstone, but there were small caves and rock outcroppings where we could hide, or ambush Geoffrey if he came for us.

I helped my new mother down the hill, her insecurity fading to a determined resilience I knew was a family trait. We had to keep moving.

The farther we moved from the cave, the more worried I became. I had a feeling in my gut that we were being followed. The bait in a trap for Gage, as Mauve had suggested. Perhaps we hadn't been chained because Geoffrey *wanted* us to escape.

Damn it.

Mind spinning with terrible thoughts, I pushed them aside and retraced every inch of ground I'd covered between the Touchstone and the cave to reach Gage. There had to be somewhere to set up an ambush.

If I died out here, I was taking that bastard with me.

16

FIRE HAD REPLACED the blood in my veins. For the first time in my life I fully understood the significance of my family bloodline, the gifts of the original royal families. Not even Bryn could keep up as I raced across the ground like the wind.

I didn't bother with a shuttle. I could scent the bastard and my mate, smell the terror pressed to the locked doors on the balcony. He'd held her there. Frightened her. Carried her away.

Von was tracking the others I'd scented, the six males who had stood by and watched the traitor hurt my mate. Torment her. Take her from me. I'd named them, known each and every one by the lingering trace they'd left behind.

"Gage. Stop!" Bryn's voice carried on the still night air, but I didn't want to stop. I needed to kill Geoffrey.

"Gage! We need a plan. If we surprise him, he might kill her." He was behind me, running full speed, an Elite Hunter in his prime, and he was right.

I stopped, my jaw clenched, power surging through my body. I could run all night. Hunt for days. Something dormant within me was awake now, awake and demanding to go to her. Find her. Save her. I'd never been this wild, this focused and out of control at the same time. This was instinct, the innate need of a Hunter to protect his mate. And thanks to my royal blood, I was the deadliest man on Everis right now.

Bryn caught up to me, and we waited a few minutes, breathing deeply as Thomar ran up to join us. Thomar's eyes were grave and I knew he felt the betrayal as deeply as I. Elon was absent, which was a blessing. If I'd seen him here, instead of protecting my sister back at the palace, I would have killed him and demand that my sister choose another mate, one who took her life and safety seriously.

"By the gods, I didn't know anyone could move that fast." Bryn was taking deep breaths, resting, his hands on his thighs as he bent over.

"He is a prince," Thomar offered, the explanation simple in his eyes.

"You know where he's taking her." Bryn tilted his head, looking up at me from the corner of his eyes.

"Yes." I did. Thomar did not know where Dani had found me, locked in that cage, beaten and burned and left for dead, but Bryn knew and, like me, recognized the terrain. "We're getting close."

"You can't just charge in there without a plan. He might kill her."

The rage boiling through me wasn't in the mood for a plan. I couldn't think past killing Geoffrey and taking my mate into my arms. "I will kill him. That is my plan."

"Great plan," Bryn said. "But I've got a better idea."

My feet were burning to move, my vision focused on the horizon. Soon I wouldn't be able to hold back the animal inside me demanding its mate. "Make it fast, Bryn. I can't hold back for long."

Bryn stood and held up his hands. "We'll split up, surround the cave, and come at it from both sides."

"Fine." Dani was out there. I could feel her now. "I'm going this way. If I find him, I will kill him."

"And if I find him?" Bryn asked.

"Save him for me."

"Done."

I took off again, Thomar following me, Bryn veering off in a slightly different direction. We were close, and I knew Bryn was taking the more direct route to the cave. I was faster. I went around the edge, over the ridge and across to the other side, farther from the palace. If Geoffrey was the patient Hunter I suspected him to be, he would be waiting for me.

But he was going to be disappointed. Dani was out here, the link between us strong, vibrant, pulling me intuitively in a direction that didn't make any sense. But I didn't argue with the instinct telling me to run to her. I couldn't. She was mine, and she needed me. Every cell in my body answered the call. My mind went quiet and I ran, moving so fast my own feet were a blur. Thomar lagged farther and farther behind, but he was young, a Hunter, and I knew he wouldn't lose the trail. He would come.

But not before I found my mate.

Moments later, I was rewarded as Dani's sweet scent carried to me on the breeze, fresh and vibrant. Alive. And not alone. My mother was with her. Thank the gods.

Moments later, I heard her whispered voice. "Come on, Mom. I've got you."

Mom?

"Thank you, honey."

I nearly tripped. Was that frail, kind voice coming from my mother?

Distracted, the attack came out of nowhere, Geoffrey's body barreling into mine from the side, knocking me into the rocks. I felt a rib crack, but I was no child to be beaten so easily. I twisted in mid-air, made sure his body struck with as much force as mine.

The explosion of sound made my mother scream, but I ignored the women. The threat was before me, I was locked in combat with the enemy, the man who'd tried to kill me, who'd threatened my family.

He'd hurt Dani.

For that alone, he would die.

The battle was short but feral, two Hunters in their prime. I knew that Dani and my mother appeared on the ridge overlooking our position, that Thomar approached, that Bryn would be here in moments, the sound of our struggle bringing him to the fight.

None of it mattered. Nothing mattered but killing Geoffrey. Ending the threat to my mate.

He pounded me with his fists, but I felt nothing, striking hard and fast, over and over. I wasn't a man. I was a predator, a Hunter. The scent of my blood and his mingled, driving me to the brink of madness.

Geoffrey threw me, his strength beyond anything I'd faced before, even in training and I hit the rocks hard, fell to the ground below. I was back on my feet in seconds. Covered in dirt, blood, rage, we circled each other.

Above us, Dani and my mother watched, safely out of his reach. He couldn't get to them without going through me.

"Don't kill him, Gage. He's your brother!" My mother's voice carried like an ion blast through the night and Geoffrey blinked, distracted. Shocked.

"You knew?" His roar of rage was deafening and my mother screamed as he leapt for them.

We collided in mid-air, my hands around his neck, twisting with a ruthlessness I barely recognized. When his bones snapped, I dropped his limp body to the dirt below me and leapt again, clearing the ridge, landing in a crouch in front of my mate.

"Dani." I had no words, I just needed to feel her. Smell her. Touch her.

She threw herself at me and I held her as she shook, as the beast that I'd become receded now that she was safe in my arms. Taking a moment to collect myself, I looked up at my mother. "Are you unharmed, Mother?"

"Yes, Son. Your Dani saved us both."

Thomar stepped into view, his gaze locked on Geoffrey's still form. I saw betrayal in his eyes, and disgust. He knelt before my mother, head bowed in shame. "Can you forgive me, my lady? I trusted him, endangered you. I am ashamed, and beg your forgiveness."

My mother scoffed and ruffled Thomar's hair like he was

a child. "Nonsense. He had us all fooled. Even Gage's father."

"He killed your father, too, Gage. He told me on the balcony. I'm so sorry." Dani's whispered confession hurt, but the sting of losing my father was nothing compared to the thought of losing her. My life. My blood. *Mine.*

Bryn reached us as I growled. The beast was back, the animal that needed his mate.

I held Dani, not letting go as Bryn called for a shuttle to pick us up and take us back to the palace. I carried Dani onboard and we left Geoffrey behind. The traitor's body would never again occupy the same space as my mate.

The moment we landed in the courtyard, Bryn opened the shuttle door. The entire palace was blazing with light, buzzing with activity. Teeming with Hunters. The party was over and it seemed every loyal Hunter who served me was on the ground, waiting to greet us. Protect us. Hover. Apologize.

Gods, I did not have time for this.

"Go," Bryn said, his eyes dark, his stance rigid. "We will see to the guards, and to your mother." He had the same adrenaline flooding his system that I did. He knew the best outlet to release it was to fuck and fuck hard. But his mate hadn't been kidnapped. Mine had. Besides the need to bleed off this excess energy, I needed to know, to feel, that Dani was alive. Whole. Safe. And having her in my arms, holding her, touching her, being buried deep within her, would eventually let that sink in.

I had no doubt that Bryn would drag Katie to their bed as soon as this mission was complete. For now, he would see it to the end, take care of Geoffrey's body, the relocation of the traitorous guards to the prison on Incar, and ensure that

Von and Elon had a new, rested squad of guards brought on for my family's protection.

Von strode forward and I felt a moment's relief at seeing him, a friend. A Hunter I trusted. "The grounds are secure, Gage. Every single room has been searched."

"And the traitors?" I could not allow the men who'd betrayed my mate to roam free this night.

"In chains." The satisfied look in Von's eyes, and the smear of blood on his cheek gave me a sense of satisfaction as well.

"I hope they resisted."

"Oh, they did indeed."

"Men are so weird." My mate's voice was soft, feminine, and totally out of place in this moment of death and darkness. Vengeance.

I looked to Dani, her once fashionably-styled hair now a wild, snarled tangle. Her golden gown was snagged and torn in spots, dirt smudged. Her makeup was gone, sweat and dust coating her skin in a sheen of brown. She'd been through so much, and yet to me, she looked stunning.

This was the real Dani. Protective. Fierce. Ruthless in her own way. She didn't need diamond dust and fancy ball gowns. She didn't need anything at all to be perfect. I needed her. Now. My cock was hard, throbbing, the excess energy engorging it with the wild need to rut.

I nodded to Von, who stood waiting. I was no longer needed here. My task was complete. My mate was at my side and safe.

"Come, Dani."

She frowned. "Where are we going?" she asked.

I didn't know exactly, just away from everyone else.

"Take my hand or I will toss you over my shoulder," I

warned. I would, too. I was in no mood for an argument. I just wanted her. Now.

She must have heard the truth of it in my tone, seen it in my direct gaze, for she closed the last few feet between us and put her hand in mine, our marks touching.

I started walking, pulling her along. The last time I had done this, she'd forced me to stop because of her injured ankle. Not this time. I didn't have to pull her for long; she was readily keeping up.

"Where are we going?" she repeated.

"The first dark corner."

"God, yes," she murmured.

I looked about, leading her down long, empty hallways I hadn't ventured in since I was a boy. I turned left, then right, spurred by her words, my cock starting to take over my thoughts. I needed to be inside her. Now. Nothing else. Must. Fuck. My. Mate.

I was turning into that caveman after all.

There! An alcove, poorly lit, no one about. And if they were, I didn't care at this point. I was fiercely protective of Dani, and while I would usually not allow anyone to see or hear her screams of pleasure, this time it didn't matter. The sound would ring out and everyone would know she was alive and whole, that her mate was taking care of her, filling her. Giving her the orgasm she needed.

Alive.

We were alive.

"This won't be gentle, mate."

"No," she repeated, her breathing ragged and not from exertion. Her pale gaze raked over me with a need that was palpable.

I walked toward her. She retreated until her back was

against the wall, her hands at her sides. I watched her chest rise and fall, her pupils dilate.

"This will be fast."

"I just want you in me," she said. "Fill me. Fuck me."

It was the first time she'd spoken so carnally. I loved it, but I wouldn't do as she wanted. Not yet. She wasn't in control here. I hadn't had it the entire time she'd been taken, but I would dominate now.

I dropped to my knees before her, gripped the hem of her skirt and lifted it above my head, diving underneath. I ripped her panties from her pussy, baring it for my pleasure. And hers.

At her gasp, I shoved the gown to her waist, looking up to see her looking down at me, watching my bold actions.

Her long, lean legs were pale in stark contrast to the dark alcove. And between them, her pussy, was like a beacon to me. The plump lips with the trimmed pubic hair were wet with her arousal. I could see it, smell it. With one quick glance up at her, I licked my lips, my mouth watering at what I was about to do.

"You'll come, mate, hard and fast. Then I'll fuck you. While I might be a caveman, I want you ready."

"I'm ready now," she replied.

I slowly shook my head. "You'll do as I say and come."

Hooking my hands about her hips, I gripped her bare ass and pulled her to me. My mouth was on her a second later. She cried out, her fingers instantly going to my head, tangling in my hair.

Her flavor exploded on my tongue. Hot, spicy, sweet. Her folds were plush and soft, her clit firming and plumping as I sucked and laved it.

I plunged two fingers into her, feeling the liquid depths

of her pussy. She was drenched for me. She hadn't been wrong when she'd said she was more than ready for my cock. Her walls rippled and clenched as I found the little ridge deep within, curled my fingers and pressed. I knew her, knew what made her gasp with desire, what would taunt and tease her to the brink of climax but not tip her over. Knew exactly where to set her off on the left side of her clit.

There was no time for the slow burn. She'd come and now. Know that I was in control, that I ruled her body, her heart and her mind. That I could do with her what I wanted, and that meant pleasure. Nothing but pleasure. Love.

Feeling.

"Gage!" she cried as I didn't relent, didn't give her any quarter. Within seconds, I had her up on her tiptoes, her fingers nearly tugging out my hair. Tensing, tensing like a bow, but I pushed her over. She melted on me as she screamed, her body writhing with the bliss I gave it. Her sounds were something I elicited from her. The juices I swallowed were a sign that her body submitted, succumbed and accepted what I gave it. And it wanted more.

I didn't wait for the spasms to stop, but left her in the throes of her passion as I stood, ripped open the front of my pants, bent my knees and thrust deep.

She cried out as I lifted her up, directly off her feet so she was impaled on my cock. I held her up with my cock buried to the hilt and the wall at her back. Her inner walls continued to milk me, this time around my cock. She was so tight, her swollen core nearly strangling it. But one deep thrust wasn't enough. I had to move, had to use her pussy to ease the ache in my balls, to soothe the frustration, the fear, the desperation I had for her.

Leaning forward, I kissed her neck, breathed in her scent as my hips shifted, thrust. Pounded.

"My mate. My love. My heart," I murmured as I fucked her hard.

She just kept saying *yes, yes, yes* over and over as I took her.

I didn't last thirty seconds. The pleasure built at the base of my spine, my balls drew up to my body and the tingle and pressure wasn't something I could hold back. I came on a growl, a nip at her neck as I groaned, filling her with pulse after thick pulse of my seed.

The pleasure was so great I saw stars, felt as if the top of my head was blowing off. I pulled from her, set her back on her feet. We were still panting, trying to catch our breaths. Dani hadn't come with me. I'd sated her once, but that wasn't enough. I needed to hear her again. I was desperate for it. For her.

I spun her about, set her hands on the wall by her head, wrapped a hand about her waist and pulled her back. Her ass was out and I could see everything, her swollen and dripping pussy, her pale thighs coated with my seed.

My cock was still rock hard, even though I'd just come, a ruddy red and angry looking. It glistened in the dim light, coated in Dani's arousal, my seed. Once wasn't enough.

I put my hand beside hers, leaned my body over hers. "Again."

"Yes," she whimpered, wiggling her hips.

I took that as invitation and filled her again.

"Gage! Fuck, you're so deep."

I was, I felt her womb nudge the head of my cock.

"You'll come, milk the seed from my balls and take it all," I breathed.

I was lost in her. God, if there was an earthquake, I'd never know. If the palace caught fire, I'd not be able to stop.

I had one mission. Make Dani come. Fill her with my seed. Make a baby. I knew this would be the time. Wild and abandoned. Nothing hidden. Inhibitions gone. In this moment, as I fucked her raw and wild, we were our true selves, our basest natures. And nothing would keep my seed from taking root.

Sweat coursed down my brow, the sound of our bodies slapping together as loud as our ragged breaths.

The pleasure was so intense, even after coming just seconds ago. She was so wet, my seed made her impossibly slick. I slid my thumb over where we were joined, felt my cock piston in and out of her, collecting our combined juices. I found her tempting ass, worked the tentative hole open until I breached it with my thumb.

I took her, pussy and ass, fucking her with my cock and digit.

Her head lifted, her hair flying down and over her back. She was wild, lost in it. So beautiful. Gorgeous in her abandon.

"Come, mate. Now," I commanded.

I felt her inner walls clench once, her body go tense, just before she cried out. Her pleasure was so great her palms slipped on the wall. I hooked my free arm about her waist, held her up, lifted her off her feet with deep thrusts, fucking her as she needed.

I followed her over, filling her with even more seed, knowing with each rhythmic pulse of her inner muscles, that she was taking it all into her womb.

She was boneless in my arms, her breathing ragged.

Carefully, I pulled from her, spun her about and pulled her into my arms. I kissed her, wild and fierce, tasted her.

Her pale eyes, hazy with passion, met mine. She smiled almost dreamily. "That's all you've got, caveman?"

My lips a fraction of an inch from hers, I shook my head. "We're not done, mate," I growled before my lips crushed hers again as I pressed her back against the wall and took her again.

17

HOLY SHIT, that had been hot. I now knew what *wild monkey sex* was. I'd had an idea, but it hadn't been anything like the real thing.

I smiled, snuggled in closer to Gage's side. My head was using his chest for a pillow. I didn't remember exactly how he got me back to our rooms. He'd kissed me the whole way, banging into walls. Doors. Neither one of us wanting to stop or come up for air.

God, he was intense. And hot. And dominant. And powerful. And mine.

He'd quickly showered us both, soaping and rinsing us of all that had happened, then tucked us into bed. He didn't make any move to take me again, only pulled me into him so we were as close as possible, my head resting on his chest, then fell promptly to sleep.

He'd spent hours trying to find us. I'd seen a blur in the darkness, moving toward our hiding place. When Geoffrey had pounced, and I realized that moving blur was Gage, I'd gasped.

I'd known Hunters were fast, but holy shit, I'd never seen anything like that. I'd never even heard of anything like that, other than in a romance novel I'd once read where the hero was a vampire.

Maybe the superhero Flash?

Maybe.

He'd been hunting, running, moving like lightning. And in all that time, I hadn't slept either. Between the monkey sex and the tenderness in the shower, I hadn't been able to keep my eyes open much longer than he did.

But now, hours later, I was awake and felt better. Rested. My mind eased knowing his arms were around me, his steady heartbeat beneath my ear.

The traitor was gone. Geoffrey. A long lost—deranged— half-brother, dead. God, just thinking about Geoffrey, how his mother had been passed over for duty and wealth, for political power, instead of love. But all sympathy for her died when I thought about what she'd done to her son. She'd given in to hatred and anger, and spread that hatred to her child like a cancer. Geoffrey had deserved better, but he didn't need to go about getting it by killing his father, for leaving Gage to die. For wanting me and Mauve dead, too.

It was too much. He'd been so far past redemption, I had to believe death was best for him. The end had been violent, but he was finally at peace.

While I doubted Geoffrey would be the last threat to Gage's life, or mine, I didn't think my mate had any more skeletons, or unknown relatives, in his proverbial closet.

Mauve, who at first I'd thought was a lunatic, wasn't half bad. Perhaps it took a kidnapping and vengeful man to put it all in perspective.

And that included how I felt for Gage. For the child I carried. I realized then that he still didn't know. I squeezed Gage, the need to hug him to me, even though I was lying on top of him, was too great to resist.

"I love you," I said aloud, though I knew he was asleep and couldn't hear. I'd say it again when he was awake, but I couldn't hold the words in any longer. They were for him, and for our son.

"I love you, too," Gage replied, startling me. I felt the rumble of the words in his chest.

Lifting my head, I looked down at him. He looked well-rested, the tension gone. In its place, a soft gaze, a tender look, a small smile.

His eyes weren't dark with need, but with a longing that went deeper than sex.

"You do?" I whispered.

"You doubt my love?" he asked in return. His hand slid down my bare back.

I thought for a moment. "No. I just hadn't heard you say the words."

"I have shown you my love with every action, every word. Every thought. Everything I do, is for you."

"You are a prince," I countered. "Everything you do is for your people."

"That would be true, but because of you, I defy convention. I may be the prince, but *he* bends to your will. I would burn the council of the Sevens to the ground if they threatened you. I am at your mercy, love."

I smiled then. "You are?"

"Of course. Completely."

I pushed up so I was sitting beside him. His gaze dropped to my bare breasts and that contented look was quickly replaced with heat.

I grabbed the sheet, tossed it toward the foot of the bed, uncovering Gage's gorgeous body down to his ankles. His cock was quickly rising to the occasion.

"Then I will have my way with you."

One dark brow went up, his hand cupping my hip. "Who has control in the bedroom?"

I harrumphed. "Not just the bedroom," I countered, thinking of how he'd dominated me in the hallway just hours ago. My pussy still ached from the fervent attention.

He grinned, wickedly, which only made me want to dominate him all the more.

"You said you are at my mercy."

He looked at me, studied me thoughtfully. His hand came up, cupped my breast, kneaded it gently.

I kept his gaze, waited, even though the caress made my pussy soften, get wet in anticipation of whatever he had planned.

He pulled his hand away, tucked it, and his other one, up behind his head, his elbows splayed out. "You wish to have your way with me?"

I nodded, licked my lips at the thought of having every hard inch of him to do with as I wished.

"Very well, do with me as you will."

It was my turn to grin. "You're still in control," I countered. "You're *letting* me have this opportunity to fuck you as I want."

His eyes went darker at my words.

"Trust me, I might be allowing it, but I will enjoy whatever you choose to do."

I wrapped my fingers around the base of his hard cock, gripped it and slid my hand up, stroking him. "Even this?"

His hips bucked automatically and he hissed out a breath. "Even that."

Oh, this was going to be fun.

Leaning forward, I swirled my tongue over the flared head, tasted the pearly drop of pre-cum. The salty tang burst across my taste buds. "Even this?" I asked again, now blatantly teasing him.

He growled, but didn't move his hands. "Even that. Take me deep, mate."

I lifted off of him, shaking my head. "You can't top from the bottom," I countered.

He frowned, not understanding the meaning of the Dominant/submissive term.

"You may say yes, more and my name. You may even beg. But that's it."

"If I agree, will you put my cock back in your mouth?"

"Yes, and I might even put your cock in my pussy, ride it until I come all over it."

He growled again, his hands moving up to grip the headboard, his knuckles going white. I could see how hard this was for him and I reveled in the power.

"You might be a prince, but I now have all the power."

"Yes, Princess," he said, then sighed, as I took him into my mouth.

"Oh, and mate?" I asked, remembering what I wanted to tell him before he'd gotten me so distracted. "You'd better behave. I speak with the power of two now."

"Oh?" he asked, his gaze fixed on my breasts.

"I am the one carrying your son, after all."

He stilled and I wasn't even sure he was breathing. His eyes lifted to mine. Held.

"What?"

I licked my lips. "Geoffrey had one of those wands, showed me the results. He wanted...well, it doesn't matter now."

"A baby?"

I nodded. "It's crazy, I know. But he showed me the scan with our baby's DNA. It's a boy. He's probably the size of a speck of dust, but he's growing inside me. Our son." I placed my hand low, over my abdomen, then grabbed Gage's hand, pressed it there. "He's real, Gage. He's growing right now. He's ours." I was overcome with happiness, tears sliding down my face. How was it even possible to be this happy?

Perhaps the idea finally clicked, but he moved his hands, gripped my hips. "Mate, you have my very heart. But how could you let me ravish you the way I did? I could have hurt the baby."

I laughed. "I'm pretty sure having hot sex won't do anything. I doubt any babies would be born otherwise."

"I am only concerned about *our* baby."

"Well, you should be concerned about our baby's mother and her need to come all over your hard cock."

His mouth fell open. I'd surprised him. I laughed, feeling happy and complete.

"I should spank your ass for your impertinence," he said, then frowned. "Will that hurt the baby?"

I didn't answer, for I realized he was going to be cautious and crazy for the next nine months. I needed to distract him before he put me in some kind of Everian bubble wrap.

"Where was I? Oh yes, your hands were on the headboard and I was in charge."

He frowned, but the way his cock pulsed, I knew he was right there with me.

Once his hands were back in place over his head, I lowered my head to his cock, took it into my mouth. I wanted his mind off of everything but this. Me. Us.

The thick heft of it stretched my lips wide and I laved it with my tongue, feeling the vein that ran up the turgid length pulse.

"Dani," he groaned in response, swelling as I continued to work him with my mouth, tongue and hand.

"Please," he groaned after a time.

I lifted off, licked my lips. Sweat dotted his brow, his jaw was clenched and every muscle in his body was rigid.

"Begging?" I asked, loving it. My pussy was wet and I was just as eager as he. "You want my pussy?"

He nodded.

"How bad?" I teased.

"Desperately."

We were playing and even in his desperate state, he allowed it to continue. And because of this, I was bold. Bolder, perhaps, than I ever knew possible.

I moved and straddled his waist, cupped my breasts.

"Very well, you shall have my pussy. After..." Instead of shimmying back and taking his cock inside me, I went up onto my knees and moved up his torso so that my wet core hovered right over his mouth.

"Make me come and then I shall consider riding your cock."

He groaned, his eyes on my pussy. He licked his lips.

"You said I needed to come, to ensure I was ready for it. It's so big and all."

His gaze met mine for the briefest of moments before he let go of the headboard, gripped my hips and pulled me down onto his face.

I was the one to hold on now. He worked me with the voraciousness of someone pushed to the brink.

"God, Gage. Yes, like that." I came within a minute. My need had been so great and his skill beyond comprehension.

I caught my breath, slid down his body so I laid on top of him, his cock nestled at my entrance, my lips on his. I tasted my essence.

"Are you ready, Prince, for your wild ride?" I asked.

He kissed me again.

His hands moved to my hips once again, worked me down and on him so I was filled completely.

"My princess, my love, the wild ride began the second we began to dream share."

And that was the last thing he said before I sat up and rode him, taking him as I wanted.

He was right. This life we now shared was the wild ride and I couldn't wait for what would come next.

EPILOGUE

"WE WILL NEED MORE rooms in the palace," Gage commented, as we entered the dining hall.

One hand was at my back, the other holding mine, as if I couldn't walk on my own. But that was my mate's way, ever protective since he'd found out I was pregnant, which had been months ago. The doctor had confirmed what Geoffrey's scan had shown. I'd gotten pregnant the very first time Gage had taken me. Now, nine months later, he was even more obsessed with my safety. Of course, I was carrying around what looked like a watermelon beneath my shirt, and I hadn't seen my feet in five weeks.

Von, Bryn and Elon all stood at our arrival out of deference to me. Their mates didn't rise. They were all quite pregnant as well. I'd found out I was pregnant first, even though Lexi and Katie had been claimed before me.

Gage had touted to the other mates that his virility was stronger than theirs. Von and Bryn took it in good stride, not caring about any kind of baby race. They were content and settled with Katie and Lexi, eager for their own babies' arrivals.

As for Elon, Gage wasn't too keen having growing proof that he'd claimed his younger sister, but they were truly mated and he had no say.

"Uncle Gage!"

A flash of a three-year old ran over to us and Gage scooped him up before he could bump into me. Gage tossed him up in the air and the boy squealed. "Again!"

He did it once more, then held him close. "Say hello to Aunt Dani."

"Hi, Aunt Dani!"

The imp looked just like Gage and my heart swelled every time they were together. It was a glimpse of what my mate would be like with our own children.

"George, let your aunt and uncle come into the room," Mauve gently scolded. She approached with a grandmotherly smile on her face. She'd been quite a hard-ass when I'd first arrived, but the discovery of a child—Geoffrey's child—had turned her into a softie.

In the aftermath of the ascension incident—that was what I called it in my mind—we'd learned so much about Geoffrey. Including the existence of George. Geoffrey had mated a woman from Feris 5 and she'd quickly become pregnant. I believed he cared for her and the child, but his obsession with revenge had clouded all of that. My arrival had been Geoffrey's proverbial last straw. In his haze of anger and retribution, he'd killed his mate, although he'd left George unscathed. Perhaps because he loved him, or perhaps because George would be his heir and carry on the bloodline, we'd never know.

I was just thankful for Geoffrey's one small mercy.

The boy was beautiful. Sweet. Impetuous and perfectly normal for a three-year old.

To say we were surprised by his existence was an understatement. Mauve took to him immediately and became his legal guardian. Since our baby was yet to be born, George was the current heir. That would change once our son made his way into the world. George was a member of the royal family, but he wasn't a legitimate son, where any children Gage and I had would be recognized as such.

Royals had rules and thousands of years of tradition.

By the way George giggled and ran to his grandmother's skirts, I knew he'd be loved and cared for. That was all that mattered.

I shifted with discomfort and Gage led me to my usual seat at the large table.

I had to hope the baby would come soon. Today would be good. As for George, he knew nothing of ascension, knew nothing but the love of his grandmother, of Gage, of all of us. I hoped he and our little one would be close friends.

George scrambled down from Gage's arms and went over to his seat, climbed up and settled. "We're having dessert for dinner!"

I glanced down at the plate before me. Sweet nut cake. My favorite.

"I asked for it," Lexi said, one hand resting on her belly. "I had a hankering."

"Hankering?" Von countered, sliding into his seat beside her, stroking his knuckles over her cheek. "Craving. And if I didn't put the request in with the cook, I'd be sleeping on the couch."

I saw Bryn blanch at the possibility. "Smart man."

"You dare scoff at a pregnant woman?" Rayla asked her mate, who'd laughed at Von and Bryn's comments.

Elon's smile slipped from his face and he held up his hands in surrender. "My love, I will eat cake every meal of the day if it keeps me in your bed."

Gage groaned.

"Cake! Cake!" George called out, putting a big piece on his fork and shoveling it in with the grace of a small child. He grinned as he chewed, crumbs on his lips.

"Like I said, we'll need more rooms in the palace soon," Gage repeated, leaning toward me after he took his seat, put his napkin in his lap.

"Four babies and a toddler will fill up the palace?" I asked. "I'm quite sure this place has several dozen empty rooms, and that's just on the second floor." Really, this place was ridiculous.

My BFFs had moved to the palace after the ascension incident. Von and Bryn had decided to shift their Hunter duties over to the royal guard. I was glad to have Katie and Lexi close by, especially now that we were all going to have babies at the same time. They'd be able to grow up together, be besties, too. And George would be the big brother to protect them all.

"That's this year," Gage countered. "Your pussy's so greedy for my cock, you'll be pregnant again within a few months."

While I didn't argue with him that I'd been ridiculously horny throughout my pregnancy, the idea of being a beached whale again so soon had me debating if I wanted birth control for a little while.

"Uncle Gage, I'm going to swim in my bathtub before bed!"

Mauve looked at the boy fondly. "All done?" she asked him.

He nodded, put his fork down. The plate was clean before him, not even a crumb.

"There's cake all over your face. It's a good thing you're off for a swim, Prince George," she said, standing and taking his hand. She called him that often enough so he'd become used to the title. Nothing more about his future or his title, but that was enough for now. As a biological heir to Gage's father, the boy really was a prince, a bastard prince, but they didn't seem to use that word on this planet, at least not in polite company, and I wasn't about to introduce it, not when the imp in question was such a joy to all of us.

Gage leaned into me as I took a bite of the delicious cake. "Don't worry, I'll get you all clean in the bath later, too."

He smiled and I knew that life couldn't get any better. A baby on the way, friends surrounding me. A doting mate. I felt like a princess. I was a princess, but to Gage, I would always be just plain Dani.

And I couldn't love him more.

Ready for more? Start *Interstellar Brides® Program: The Colony* series with Surrender to the Cyborgs!

Wrongly imprisoned whistle-blower Rachel Pierce would

rather take her chances with her court appeal than accept her place as the first Interstellar Bride destined for the Colony. She's stubborn and determined to seek justice—and her freedom—on Earth...but her mates are not willing to risk her life or her future on a system they believe to be both primitive and corrupt.

Maxim of Prillon Prime fought ten long years in the Hive wars. Captured and tortured with his second, Ryston, they escaped only to be rejected by their own people and condemned to life on the Colony with the other "contaminated" cyborg warriors. As leader of Sector 3, it's Maxim's duty to set an example for his warriors and summon a bride. When she refuses transport, he can't allow her rejection to demoralize an entire planet of battle hardened but jaded warriors. Maxim and Ryston transport to Earth where they decide she's theirs and a maximum security human prison will not keep them apart.

Getting Rachel to the Colony is only the first challenge they will face. Convincing their beautiful mate to surrender to not one, but two dominant warriors is another. Even if they can win her love, a new evil is rising on the Colony and someone close to Maxim will be its first victim. Maxim will be its second, unless Rachel's love and relentless pursuit of the truth proves strong enough to save him.

Click here to read Surrender to the Cyborgs now!

A SPECIAL THANK YOU TO MY READERS...

Want more? I've got *hidden* bonus content on my web site *exclusively* for those on my mailing list.

If you are already on my email list, you don't need to do a thing! Simply scroll to the bottom of my newsletter emails and click on the *super-secret* link.

Not a member? What are you waiting for? In addition to ALL of my bonus content (great new stuff will be added regularly) you will be the first to hear about my newest release the second it hits the stores—AND you will get a free book as a special welcome gift.

Sign up now! http://freescifiromance.com

FIND YOUR INTERSTELLAR MATCH!

YOUR mate is out there. Take the test today and discover your perfect match. Are you ready for a sexy alien mate (or two)?

VOLUNTEER NOW!

interstellarbridesprogram.com

DO YOU LOVE AUDIOBOOKS?

Grace Goodwin's books are now available as
audiobooks...everywhere.

LET'S TALK SPOILER ROOM!

Interested in joining my **Sci-Fi Squad**? Meet new like-minded sci-fi romance fanatics and chat with Grace! Get excerpts, cover reveals and sneak peeks before anyone else. Be part of a private Facebook group that shares pictures and fun news! Join here:

https://www.facebook.com/groups/scifisquad/

***

Want to talk about Grace Goodwin books with others? Join the **SPOILER ROOM** and spoil away! Your GG BFFs are waiting! (And so is Grace)

Join here:

https://www.facebook.com/groups/ggspoilerroom/

GET A FREE BOOK!

JOIN MY MAILING LIST TO BE THE FIRST TO KNOW OF NEW RELEASES, FREE BOOKS, SPECIAL PRICES AND OTHER AUTHOR GIVEAWAYS.

http://freescifiromance.com

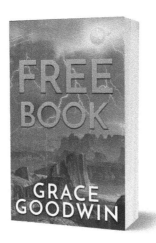

ALSO BY GRACE GOODWIN

Interstellar Brides® Program

Mastered by Her Mates

Assigned a Mate

Mated to the Warriors

Claimed by Her Mates

Taken by Her Mates

Mated to the Beast

Tamed by the Beast

Mated to the Vikens

Her Mate's Secret Baby

Mating Fever

Her Viken Mates

Fighting For Their Mate

Her Rogue Mates

Claimed By The Vikens

The Commanders' Mate

Matched and Mated

Hunted

Viken Command

The Rebel and the Rogue

Interstellar Brides® Program: The Colony

Surrender to the Cyborgs

Mated to the Cyborgs

Cyborg Seduction

Her Cyborg Beast

Cyborg Fever

Rogue Cyborg

Cyborg's Secret Baby

Her Cyborg Warriors

Interstellar Brides® Program: The Virgins

The Alien's Mate

His Virgin Mate

Claiming His Virgin

His Virgin Bride

His Virgin Princess

Interstellar Brides® Program: Ascension Saga

Ascension Saga, book 1

Ascension Saga, book 2

Ascension Saga, book 3

Trinity: Ascension Saga - Volume 1

Ascension Saga, book 4

Ascension Saga, book 5

Ascension Saga, book 6

Faith: Ascension Saga - Volume 2

Ascension Saga, book 7

Ascension Saga, book 8

Ascension Saga, book 9

Destiny: Ascension Saga - Volume 3

Other Books

Their Conquered Bride

Wild Wolf Claiming: A Howl's Romance

ABOUT GRACE

Grace Goodwin is a USA Today and international bestselling author of Sci-Fi and Paranormal romance with more than one million books sold. Grace's titles are available worldwide in multiple languages in ebook, print and audio formats. Two best friends, one left-brained, the other right-brained, make up the award-winning writing duo that is Grace Goodwin.

They are both mothers, escape room enthusiasts, avid readers and intrepid defenders of their preferred beverages. (There may or may not be an ongoing tea vs. coffee war occurring during their daily communications.) Grace loves to hear from readers!

All of Grace's books can be read as sexy, stand-alone adventures. But be careful, she likes her heroes hot and her love scenes hotter. You have been warned...

www.gracegoodwin.com
gracegoodwinauthor@gmail.com

Lightning Source UK Ltd.
Milton Keynes UK
UKHW021433030321
379713UK00008B/2166

9 781795 901734